Coltan

First published by O Books, 2009
O Books is an imprint of John Hunt Publishing Ltd., The Bothy, Deershot Lodge, Park Lane, Ropley,
Hants, SO24 0BE, UK
office1@o-books.net
www.o-books.net

Distribution in:	South Africa
	Alternative Books
UK and Europe	altbook@peterhyde.co.za
Orca Book Services	Tel: 021 555 4027 Fax: 021 447 1430
orders@orcabookservices.co.uk	
Tel: 01202 665432 Fax: 01202 666219	Text copyright Alberto Vázquez-Figueroa 2008
Int. code (44)	Cover: Marc Armangue
USA and Canada	Design: Stuart Davies
NBN	
custserv@nbnbooks.com	ISBN: 978 1 84694 210 5
Tel: 1 800 462 6420 Fax: 1 800 338 4550	

Australia and New Zealand
Brumby Books
sales@brumbybooks.com.au
Tel: 61 3 9761 5535 Fax: 61 3 9761 7095

Far East (offices in Singapore, Thailand,
Hong Kong, Taiwan)
Pansing Distribution Pte Ltd
kemal@pansing.com
Tel: 65 6319 9939 Fax: 65 6462 5761

The rights of Alberto Vázquez-Figueroa as
author have been asserted in accordance with
the Copyright, Designs and Patents Act 1988.

A CIP catalogue record for this book is available
from the British Library.

Artwork by Amanda Robinson at www.amandadesign.co.uk
© Cover Image: Getty Images
Translated by Vicky Collier

www.albertovazquezfigueroa.com
Translation copyright Desperado Management, London

Printed by Digital Book Print

Coltan

Alberto Vázquez-Figueroa

BOOKS

Winchester, UK
Washington, USA

Houston, 2007

All fourteen members of the board of directors had taken a seat, one by one, around the enormous table. Now they waited to hear what their austere president, who had called on them with quite uncharacteristic urgency, had to tell them.

"As the government of the United States looks set to withdraw from Iraq, leaving behind it a trail of death and destruction that has torn the country apart, we have decided that the company responsible for this cruel and destructive disaster –DallJHouston, of which you are the main shareholders – must now return the profits reaped from this atrocious and barbaric act of aggression.

"Of course it is not possible to bring back the dead, but it may be possible to repair some of the damage done. We are therefore demanding that from your profits, you now return at least one hundred billion dollars to us.

"If you do not meet with this reasonable request, we will execute one of you, every two weeks, no matter what protective measures you might take or where you hide.

"Do not doubt the gravity of what I say, proof of which may be found in the absence of Richard Marzan, the only colleague on the board of directors who is not present. You can find him inside one of the earthenware jars that adorn the garden of his lavish mansion on the shores of the river.

"If you decide to cooperate we will send you a list of the hospitals, schools, buildings, bridges and roads that you must start to build immediately.

"If you do not comply, then by the end of the summer only two of you will remain, and that time itself will be brief.

"Blood money will be cleansed with blood.

" Aarohum Al Rashid."

Very carefully, Peter Corkenham placed the document on the table as if it might burn his fingers, and looking at each one whilst cleaning his glasses, said with seasoned calm:

"This morning Richard's body was removed from one of the earthenware jars. His throat had been slit yesterday afternoon…"

"But who is this 'Aarohum Al Rashid?'" said an anonymous but clearly agitated voice. " A new Osama Bin Laden?"

"I have no idea, but he has evidently taken his name from the leading sultan in *One Thousand and One Nights*," the president said. "We should think of him as the hero of the story, while we can assume the roles of the forty thieves."

"What nonsense!"

"I doubt it felt like that for Richard," he replied sharply. "Or his wife and children."

"Do you mean to say that we are faced with a real-life assassin?" said the same voice.

"As far as I can tell."

"A terrorist?" Bem Sandorf, the Californian sitting almost opposite him at the other end of the table, asked.

The increasingly disgruntled president of Dall&Houston stretched out his hands, palms pushed forward, as if to halt any further questions from any of his colleagues sitting around the table. He cleared his throat several times and sipped on a glass of water before speaking:

"Terrorists are usually people that aim to destroy, not rebuild, so the first case scenario we must consider, following this unusual proposal, is that we are being deliberately misled. They are not demanding money or the release of criminal associates. They are asking that we return the money that we have earned in Iraq by rebuilding its schools and hospitals, which I am sure you will all agree, is a type of ransom that's as yet quite unheard of."

"It's still a form of blackmail," Sandorf insisted. "The end doesn't justify the means."

"I don't think your comments are quite appropriate at the

moment," Jeff Hamilton, the New Yorker sitting to the right of the president, said harshly. "We all, around this table, know that certain decisions taken by us led directly to the outbreak of war which we were then unable get out of," he paused as if to punctuate an idea that was simply not open to discussion. "Or maybe we just want to try and avoid, at least amongst ourselves, any hint of hypocrisy, since we are now confronted with the painful truth that in one way or another we are in fact being brought to account by these people."

"With what right?" Gus Callow asked.

"With the same right, more or less, that this very board of directors had to make the decisions it made," Hamilton replied in an acidic tone. "That is to say, none."

"I do believe, however, that in our case..."

"Enough!" ruled Peter Corkenham with absolute authority. "I do not intend to spend the day discussing past glories or mistakes. Jeff, you are right, the facts are clear and we are faced with a somewhat unpleasant situation..." he turned his head from left to right, observing the faces of his employees and said, "Any suggestions?"

"To accept it," said Judy Slander, as timidly as ever.

"Unacceptable, my dear. We cannot ask thousands of share-holders to give up their dividends for the sake of saving the skin of a few directors. They would send us to the dogs and with good reason. I wouldn't dare."

"Try and negotiate a less onerous deal," Jeff Hamilton intervened once again, but this time with a markedly more conciliatory tone.

"What kind of figure were you thinking of?"

"Twenty billion."

"Also out of the question," came his firm response. "We will need all available capital for a new operation, which I will tell you about in a moment. I think it's highly unlikely that the terrorists would accept a lesser deal. Once they start negotiating with lives they are generally not inclined to further bargaining. Am I making myself clear?"

"Absolutely."

"Any other ideas?"

"Find out who it is and try and finish them off before he does us."

"Brilliantly stupid, my dear Judy," the president muttered contemptuously. "One hundred per cent of all Iraqis, seventy per cent of all Americans, and I guess about half of all citizens worldwide blame Dall&Houston for the start of this war and the worst of it is, is that they are right. Our strategy to go ahead was, at the time, clear as day for every one of us around this table, and I don't remember any of you stamping your feet, rejecting it out of hand or storming out of the room."

"That was the case."

"So we must accept that most people out there want our heads, and one of those guys is Al Rashid, who despite his ridiculous nickname, is a killer and ready to kill. To look for him would be like searching for a needle in a haystack."

"So basically we're all dead in six months?" Jeff Hamilton concluded in a gloomy tone.

"This is what I am afraid of."

"And what use will all our money be to us then?"

"Hell, you've got it in one!" exclaimed Eladio Medrano, another distressed member of the all-powerful Dall&Houston board of directors. "Our achievements mean absolutely nothing if we can't even protect ourselves from a simple assassin."

"Maybe we could get a contract with Blackwater. If the government has been using them in Iraq, I imagine they could be used to protect us here."

"Well if they have the same success rate as they do in Iraq, then we're finished," Jeff Hamilton muttered contemptuously. "They claim to be 'the best private army in the world', they cost a fortune, but they let half a dozen of our best engineers in

Baghdad get killed."

"Houston is not Baghdad."

"Well if we can transform Baghdad into the state it's in now all the way from Houston, I wouldn't be surprised if they plan to send Houston to hell, all the way from Baghdad. At least hell for all of us gathered here."

Peter Corkenham turned to face Jeff Hamilton with a pleading expression:

"I can tell that you don't like them, but because I know you are keen to do things to help this company, and bearing in mind that you have experience in this area, I would like you to draw up a report on Blackwater as soon as possible."

Colorado, 2007

Solitude found Salka Embarek and became her inseparable companion when a missile destroyed her house and killed her entire family, on the night the invasion of Iraq began. But solitude became desperation when it suddenly dawned upon her how a series of absurd decisions had led to the predicament she now found herself in; stranded on a slip road off an American highway.

As the cars, bikes and trucks whizzed past her eyes, she just sat there, trying to make some sense of the many mistakes she had made since the idea occurred to her that she must avenge the people that had nearly destroyed her in such an unjust and cruel way. It was now dawning on her that she had become just another victim of an unjust war, a puppet ready to be manipulated by whoever happened to be around to take advantage of her hatred, which in the end had little or nothing to do with the disappearance of her family.

She now had to admit to herself that she had behaved like an idiot, letting a band of conspirators with no scruples drag her here and there, dazzling her with ideas of becoming a valiant terrorist and of bringing the guilty party to justice.

They had recruited her from the rubble of Baghdad city, trained her to take on the guise of a simple middle-class English girl, they had taken her halfway across the world until she arrived in the heart of North America, and just as she had decided that she would sacrifice her life in order to create a veritable catastrophe amongst her enemies, she was abandoned in the middle of this unknown country.

There had been many like her before; those who had taken their own life, sometimes driven by rage and sometimes by a blind faith in the divine ruling that the infidels must be annihilated at all cost, so she would never understand why, having resolutely made the decision to die killing, they had abandoned her.

She thought seriously for a moment about throwing herself under one of the huge, roaring trucks that drove passed her at surprising speed, only two meters away from where she sat. It would be one solution to the endless doubts and problems she now faced; but being flattened on a lost highway on the other side of the world was not really a very dignified end for someone who had abandoned Iraq with the singular goal of blowing up a dozen or so Yankees.

So far she had not blown up a single one.

Not even hurt one.

Or even scared one.

Her terrorist training now seemed like a complete waste of time, in a country where any old student could get hold of a machine gun and carry out a high school massacre. She would not have been able to defend herself against the advances of some drunken tramp since she did not even have a penknife to her name.

She remained motionless, sitting on the small wall for about an hour, until a dilapidated truck covered in mud stopped next to her on the slip road, and a balding, red headed, unpleasant-looking man, smelling of farms, beer and sweat, got out and asked her curtly:

"How much for a blowjob?"

"What did you say?" she asked, thinking she had misunderstood.

"I said how much for a blowjob?" the repulsive man repeated grumpily. "Just a quick one in those bushes over there."

"Go to hell!" she blurted out, offended. "Who the hell do you think you are?"

"Well what do you want me to believe, sat there like a tart on the edge of the road, you imbecile. Go fuck yourself!"

After a while she realized that the stinking redhead had every right to have made a mistake. She had already seen hundreds of half-naked women hanging around the highways on the pull for desperate clients. It was not anyone else's fault that he had mistaken her for a prostitute. She decided to leave the road and buried herself in a maize field nearby that concealed her body from the chest down.

At midday as the heat pressed down on her, she decided to lie down in the undergrowth, tired, hungry, thirsty and covered in sweat.

As she lay there, troubled thoughts of what lay before her raced around her head. What on earth was an Iraqi girl with a false passport, unsure whether the police were after her not, going to do, alone in the heart of North America.

Habana, 1936

"MRE"... Mauro Rivero Elgosa. "MRE"... Mauro Rivero Elgosa. Mauro Rivero Elgosa..."MRE". Mauro Rivero Elgosa... "MRE".

From the age of three he knew how to write his name in perfect script, with long, clean, almost gothic lines, and at five years of age he could write in every script, he could copy his mother's, his teachers' and his class mates' signatures with such precision that by the time he was ten years old, his best friend, Emiliano Céspedes, was convinced that he already had a brilliant career as a forger ahead of him.

In the same way that some human beings are born with a special talent for music, painting, literature or handicrafts, Mauro Rivero Elgosa was born with the extraordinary gift of being able to copy any handwriting, any type of expression and anybody's voice, the latter of which he did especially well, even female ones, which was without doubt the result of his remarkable and unswerving powers of observation.

Unsociable and quiet, he moved like a shadow amongst shadows, always conscious of what was going on around him, while his mother, who was the only one that really knew him, thought of him as a giant sponge that only gave back a small part of the vast amount that he chose to absorb at any given moment.

He was interested in everything and everything caught his attention, while his capacity to process all this information was remarkable. At the same time, however, nothing particular seemed to grab his attention, to the extent that he was interested as much in physics one day as he was in geography, astronomy or mathematics the next.

One of the few teachers that took a degree of interest in him was Don Teofilo Arana, who was almost as grey and inaccessible as he was. He would often tease his pupil about his inability to show a preference for any subject, or make a decision that might determine a certain direction or career path, by repeating over and over again the old adage: "A Jack of all trades but a master at none."

"Talent is like water," he would say, "once spilled then it is of no use to anyone, but when it is concentrated and one drop after another falls on to the same place, the rocks are blessed."

The boy's reply took him by surprise.

"Water gets bored when it falls over and over again on to the same point, but once spilled it is free to search out new cracks into which it might slip, which alleviates that boredom."

What is written in stone, however, or at least appears that way, is that childhood and puberty are the defining moments that tend to shape a human being's destiny. In Mauro Rivero's case, these defining years were set in colorful, suffocating, noisy, rowdy and crazy Havana, where he stood out like a sad and pensive black sheep amidst a happy and carefree herd. It was hard to believe that this misplaced person would end up twisting the conventional form, which on first appearances he appeared to accept almost submissively, into such destructive and violent forces, into revolution and rebellion.

And the key to this apparent contradiction in terms lay in the fact that Mauro Rivero Elgosa had no creed, faith, social or political conviction or capacity to love anything that was not directly related to himself and his own initials: "MRE".

Nothing, beyond the end of his nose and well-manicured fingernails, mattered to him.

Not even his mother.

Marie Elgosa de Rivero, abandoned by her husband when Mauro was still a baby, had dedicated her life to working twelve-hour days in order to give her son a good start in life. In exchange for these sacrifices she received a modicum of respect and from time to time some gratitude, but never once did she enjoy his affection.

It was not long before she realized that she had brought a child into the world that might as well have been made of marble.

Soft to the touch, exquisite in form and at first glance malleable; but in reality, distant, inaccessible and cold; a kid glove that hid underneath it a fist of steel, always ready to land a brutal and unexpected punch.

Where did he come from?

A difficult question and one to which Marie never found the answer, partly because she knew very little about the family of her flighty husband, a traveling salesman, obsessed with gambling.

Santiago Rivero got a lot more pleasure out of playing dice, cards, laying money on chicken fights, greyhounds, horses, and any other form of betting, than he did from the third-rate products he used to sell, which meant that he was often obliged to disappear, leaving behind a hungry family and a rosary of IOUs that were not worth the paper they were written on.

It took his wife three years to pay off his debts in order to avoid the house being taken away and to put an end to malicious chatter, which she achieved not only from the sales of the beauty products that she had so painstakingly made, but from the sale of her own undeniable beauty, which she would hire out for hours at a time.

It was not just hearsay but the truth that on the day she closed the door to the last of her creditors she never opened the door to another man again, despite the fact that many of them who called by had only the most honorable intentions in mind.

Mauro used to accompany her to the fields to help her collect the flowers and plants that she would later grind down in palm oil and to which she would add her secret and "magical" formulas and bottle up into a variety of potions. She sold them to the mixed-race women from Havana's old town at a decent price, which earned her just enough money to keep the family home from falling down.

Under a brick in the kitchen she hid a battered book with an oilcloth covering, where she had written down in great detail all the ingredients that made up her concoctions, which, she often warned her son, would be the only thing he would inherit along with the crumbling walls that surrounded them.

"Always remember that there will be women and above all women who will try to appear more attractive to you than in reality they are," she would say over and over again. "If you concentrate on making up a good cream, you can live your life honorably without hurting anyone.

Mauro Rivero could not imagine himself running through nearby fields for the rest of his life, searching for primary materials that were often hard to come by. His incredible ability to retain knowledge, however, meant that he could imitate and on occasion even improve on the complex techniques that his mother used.

Becoming a cosmetics manufacturer was certainly not part of his plans, although the fact of the matter was that he did not have any plans at all.

By the time he had reached fifteen years of age he had learned many things and he had also reached the conclusion that man would never be the master of his own future but that it was the future that guided him day by day, nudging him in one direction or another.

Los Angeles, 2007

The Californian Bem Sandorf had invested most of the money he had earned from his substantial share-holding in Dall&Houston in buying land and vineyards, and the wine he now produced from Bodegas Sandorf enjoyed widespread fame and prestige and could be found on the shelves of the country's finest restaurants.

After leaving the board room, where he had been notified that his life, or his fortune – which to him now represented one and the same thing – were under threat, he boarded his private jet to Los Angeles where he barricaded himself into his estate and ordered his head of staff to triple the number of armed security guards in order to ensure that nobody, absolutely nobody! would be able to trespass on the grounds of his beautiful Sandorf estate.

It takes a clever man to amass a fortune like his from virtually nothing, and Sandorf was fully aware that at one time or another the decisions he had taken during his time as one of Dall&Houston's top executives might well be dragged up for judgment.

But it was one thing to be brought to justice by a genuine team of lawyers and another to be put on trial by an avenging madman who was threatening to convert his fabulous Californian cellars into dirty Iraqi hospitals.

He was wholly convinced that sooner or later the company would ensure that the cretin who called himself Aarohum Al Rashid was captured, but since it was impossible to guess at how long this might take, he decided that the best way to deal with it was by buttoning down the hatches, staying put and waiting to see what happened next.

It was also possible that the whole story was nothing more than a red herring, a cover up for the real reason that Richard Mazan, a known cocaine addict, was assassinated. It was well known that his wife had been having an affair with a South American racing driver who was something of a celebrity and that with the inheritance money she would be able to buy her handsome friend a hundred of the world's fastest racing cars.

He still preferred to err on the safe side, however, so on the Thursday exactly two weeks after Richard's death, he put a 38-caliber revolver in his pocket, just in case.

It was mid-morning when, after having checked that everything was calm and that his security guards were present and correct, acknowledging them with a slight nod of his head, he decided to venture down into the darkness of his gigantic cellar where his prize concoctions sat steadily aging.

That was the last time he was seen alive.

Forty-eight hours later the police received information that, in so many words, Ben Sandorf's body had been found fermenting inside barrel number one hundred and fourteen.

Three days later the press got hold of a copy of the strange missive that a mysterious individual who went under the name of "Aaraohum Al Rashid" had sent to Dall&Houston's executive board.

Public opinion split immediately into two almost irreconcilable camps: those that believed it was only fair that the money, which had been so cruelly and illegally obtained, should be returned to the Iraqi people, and those that dismissed it as a spineless form of blackmail that used terror tactics and assassination threats to intimidate its targets.

The debate unleashed a torrent of print and words and images span hot of the press revealing more publicly than ever before, the damage that this absurd war had done to Iraq and its people. There was not a reader or onlooker to be found that did not hold an opinion on the subject.

Could Al Rashid be compared with the legendary Robin Hood, who robbed the rich to help the poor, or was he the latest addition to the Al Qaeda movement?

Was it morally correct that those who had become rich from the blood of others should be left untried or should they be subjected to the radical method of execution without trial or defense?

Would Justice itself have even been strong enough at the time to punish all those people who had played their part, but remained hidden behind company acronyms and who, even if exposed would have employed the country's teams of top lawyers to ensure that each legal hearing was dragged out to eternity?

It was true that the majority of people had started to tire of the overwhelming power that these tycoons held, these magnates who had set themselves up as the authentic dictators of a new world order that went under the banner of globalization. Of course, most of the press and media were owned by those very same tycoons, which meant that the balance of opinion was generally set straight by them anyway.

Compared with the last century, which had followed the hegemony of fascism or communism, as the nations swung wildly to the radical left or the extreme right, this new one was taking a more subtle, though no less efficient path, dictated more by stock exchange fluctuations than the opinions of the masses. In the face of this new world order, the masses were, indeed, becoming increasingly powerless to act, surrounded by these hidden and faceless forces that now dictated their futures, the days of wild strikes and bloody revolutions were seemingly long gone.

The anonymous company directors and the share packets held in the hands of impersonal "pension funds," made it that much harder to point the finger and cry "off with their heads".

The fact, therefore, that somebody was actively trying to bring these normally invisible heads to the block signaled that change was afoot.

Colorado, 2007

She left the cornfield that afternoon and tried to make a bit more progress along the winding back roads. As evening drew in she eventually reached a lay-by, where she found a dilapidated old restaurant that stood next to an equally dilapidated and dirty motel. For a long while she just sat and watched the coming and going of cars and lorries, which soon made her realize this was not an appropriate place for a lone female to be, but she was so hungry, disorientated and exhausted that she had no option but to go to the motel and ask for a room, which they asked her to pay for in advance.

The place was dirty, rancid and depressing.

She had supper in the dirty, rancid and depressing restaurant, taking no notice of the comments being made by a group of peasant renegades that seemed to have confused her for a prostitute, before she finally took to her rickety old bed, but not before she had barricaded the door with locks and chains.

She could not believe that this was really what had become of her; that this was what lay ahead. Wandering lost through a country she hated did not bode well, especially as one day somebody might well clock her as the aspiring and stupid terrorist she was and there would be no way on earth she could explain herself and prove otherwise, so far from her home in Iraq.

Over and over again she cursed herself for having behaved in such a infantile and absurd way, and time and time again she tried to justify her decision to sacrifice herself by reasoning that at the time she had just been a bitter and lost adolescent.

She had grown up as fast as weeds on an untended patch of land, since then, quite aware of how the horrors of war had cut short her youth and how she would carry the suffering she had experienced, well into her old age.

To witness so many people dying around her; boys growing

into men before their time; men becoming old men in the blink of an eye.

During those awful years in Baghdad, someone else's death could just as quickly become your own. Dead bodies lay everywhere, dumped in the rubbish or hung from street lamps and Salka Embarek had lived in fear that one day she would turn a corner and become just another one of those bloody cadavers that had been left to the dogs.

Human beings can get used to anything; including a life without hope.

Her sleep was fretful and interrupted by horrendous nightmares that made her start with fear, over and over again. It was mid-morning when she finally decided to call the telephone number of the only person that had shown her any kindness since she had arrived in North America.

When she heard the friendly voice of the old women on the other end of the line she enquired, "Mary Lacombe...? It's me, the girl that you met a few days ago who you went fishing with. Do you remember me?"

"Oh, of course I remember you my dear!" came her immediate response. "We spent a charming day together didn't we? How are you?"

"To be honest, I'm not so good. I don't know anyone here and I don't know where to turn."

"Where are you?"

"In a road motel not far from where we met."

"Give me the address and I'll come and get you."

"There's no need for you to go to any trouble," the girl protested immediately. "We can meet wherever you say. I can get it together to come to you."

"It's no trouble, darling. I'll be there tomorrow and I promise you we will go fishing for trout in a fabulous spot that I know of, where my late husband used to go and that nobody knows about. Let's go and fish some more trout!"

thing all right again, turning it back into one of those regular nights when they would go down to the jetty for some fresh air, to make jokes and share a bottle of rum they had managed to buy after scraping together a few cents.

The three of them were quite aware that this bit of water was frequented by hungry sharks, who would already be feasting on the unfortunate Patuco.

"And if his family starts looking for him?"

"Let them look for him. I'm not going to say a word to anyone and I imagine that you guys won't be saying anything either."

"We owe you one."

"I know!" he said in his monotone voice, the tone of voice he used most of the time, only on this occasion his play mates had the strange feeling that those two short words meant the beginning of a much longer commitment. They had just become indebted to someone who they knew would never forget.

Mauro Rivero did not forgot it, but neither did he ever mention the unfortunate incident of the unhappy Patuco again, even when half of Old Havana was up in arms at the discovery of a human leg, found floating in the port.

He even managed to smile when the nitwit Bruno "The knave" said with a strange sarcasm:

"Somebody must have ended up a cripple round here."

The first criminal offence, like the first love, the first personal success, or indeed any of life's turning points that constitute important markers in the story of any human being, were of little relevance to Mauro Rivero. The fact that he was able to throw a still warm body to the sharks with such nonchalance bore testimony to this.

He used to throw empty bottles into the sea almost every night and watch them for a few moments as they were pushed out by the current along the pier and out to the port, in what had become a kind of ritual before he turned in for the night. But on that evening, when the bottles were switched for a human being, his pulse rate had not registered any change whatsoever.

In truth, nothing altered his pulse rate at all, since he was always hot.

And it was only ever, on those rare occasions, when the usually stifling Havana heat registered a fall, that Mauro Rivero would fail to turn up for an appointment.

That was the only trait he had inherited from his mother.

Marie Elgosa had been forced to leave her native Saint Etienne at a very young age, mainly due to the fact that most of her family suffered from a genetic defect called the "Raynaud Syndrome", which was an annoying, painful, rare and little-known disease that afflicted all of their lives.

Not able to stand it and fearful of ending up like her own mutilated father, who was already in a wheelchair, Maria scraped together enough money to take her south and one fine day just took off, without saying a word to anyone.

She went looking for the sun and found it in Cuba.

Life on the island had been tough, that much she could not deny, but still not comparable to the torture she would have suffered in a colder climate, where her hands and feet would have turned blue with the first frosts and where she would have lived in fear of getting gangrene, which in extreme cases could lead to amputation.

Maybe Mauro Rivero's character was a direct consequence of this illness that had affected him since birth and dictated his behavior in much the same way as being born blind, death or disabled would have done so.

Was it possible that his character had been shaped by the fact that his capillaries were incredibly sensitive to the slightest drop in temperature?

If every time that his hands or feet went blue he was overcome with terrible pain, until his blood started to move around normally once again, it was logical that as a young child he would have created defense mechanisms that worked to minimize this pain.

And nobody else would know how efficient or powerful these mechanisms were, given the fact that nobody else could determine how intense the pain was that he felt.

No one had invented a thermometer that could measure pain levels, especially since no two human beings would develop an illness in the same way. The disease never presented itself as a logical reaction to a determined aggression, nor did it respond to any predetermined parameters.

The level of pain experienced would depend a lot on the individual person and their mood at that time.

As a child, Mauro was able to spend hours on the beach, lying under an inclement tropical sun without a drop of sweat appearing anywhere on his body, but he could not spend more than five minutes in the sea, however hot he may have been.

While he remained immobile, as if absent, his eyes half shut, observing his friends splashing around in the sea, his mind remained active, as if all the energy he was saving by not moving around was being channeled into some kind of personal meditation.

Blackwater

"Blackwater" does not operate within the confines of any prevailing law, either here or abroad, and appears to have close and direct links with the far right radical Christian party. They tend to use automatic weapons capable of firing 900 bullets a minute and are called in for special missions like street-patrol on the streets of new Orleans in the aftermath of hurricane Katrina or as bodyguards for important government officials in Baghdad.

The "company" has a military base and a fleet of twenty or so airplanes and claims to be able to put 20,000 men on the ground in just a few days.

In March 2004, four of its members were assaulted, lynched, cauterized and burnt by a mob of enraged Iraqis in the predominantly Sunni city of Fallujah. Their bodies were hung from a bridge over the Euphrates and the retaliation carried out by their brothers in arms only served to further increase Iraqi resistance that now terrorizes both the civilian population and American soldiers.

The "company", which has been brought in to question by the law and is generally despised by the general public, saw some of its members greeted in Washington as if they were the new heroes in the fight against terrorism.

The manager and owner of the outfit, Erik Prince, considers his empire to be the equivalent to America's fifth military arm. This is not, however, some regular kind of army but a powerful militia of mercenaries, the likes of which have not been seen since Roman times. The George Bush Administration has secretly been financing it to operate in areas of international conflict, including on American soil. A report published by the United Nations Committee revealed that with the privatization of the war "private or independent contractors" have, for some industrialized countries become their primary export into regions of armed conflict. The United Nations has expressed concern with regard to the formulas being drawn up by these private security firms that actually create these armies or conflict forces that operate outside of the law and in contravention of international law, that is to say "the Convention against the Use of Mercenaries, 1989". Every year Blackwater bills the Pentagon for hundreds of millions of dollars for services contracted, which include American spy contracts and police forces training programs carried out around the world. President Bush counts on them in his "global war on terror" since they have their own military base and troops ready to move in at any given time. Its biggest supporters are Dick Cheney, ex-Secretary of Defense Donald Rumsfeld and Coffer Black , known by some as the ex chief of the CIA's clandestine operations and currently vice-president of Blackwater.

The Administration defines the company as "a revolution in military affairs", according to the prestigious magazine "The Nation" – while many see it as a direct threat to American democracy.

Blackwater's directors defend their position against these accusations and stand proud of their image as modern mercenaries. Being a private militia, the Bush Administration is politically cagey when it comes to releasing information on their activities…and its casualties. Some 780 "private soldiers" have died in Iraq, but these are not included in the official lists of American deaths, they do not receive medical attention from the Pentagon and nobody controls their spending. Some congress members have expressed their concern with regard to the existence of these mercenary armies, but they have proved impossible to investigate.

Peter Corkenham placed the "report" on the table and rubbed his eyes for a long time before asking:

"Do you think they are capable of protecting us?"

"General opinion is that they are the best of the lot," Jeff Hamilton said casually.

"But does being able to fire off a round of 900 bullets a minute make you more efficient than someone who makes less noise but thinks more?" he persisted.

"If the issue here you're referring to is to unmask this Al Rashid, then I'd say that those animals aren't the best choice then, but I guess they might be able to protect us from being hunted down."

"I get the impression that this is going to be a confrontation between brute force and intelligence and I don't like it. I don't like it at all!"

"Looking at it from that perspective neither do I," said the other speaker, who appeared to hold a very clear opinion on the subject, "But I don't think that one thing should exclude the other. We have the means to hire Blackwater to protect us and to hire someone at the same time who is capable of finding out who this madman is."

"If he was a mad man I wouldn't be so worried," his boss countered in his typically serious and circumspect tone. "Mad men make mistakes, but something tells me deep down that this son of a bitch is not going to make any false moves, not even if we trip him up."

"Are you scared?"

"Aren't you?"

"Of course! I'm not that fond of sleeping in a bunker, turning round every minute to check there isn't anyone standing behind me with a machete in their hand. It's no way to live. Jesus Christ, this is no way to no live!"

Democratic Republic of Congo, 2007

They had promised Marcel Valerie that Bukavu was one of the most beautiful cities in the Congo, with a magnificent climate, landscaped gardens surrounding the proud mansions that lined the shores of a stunning lake, all reminiscent of its splendid past as a colonial capital.

What he actually found there was quite the opposite and quite repellent. A suffocating heat hung over the sprawl of ruined buildings that lined the narrow streets, which had been taken over by starving dogs. To make matters worse the place was overpopulated with peasants, immigrants who had been forced out of their homes by never-ending and bloody tribal wars and who descended in their hoards on the city in search of refuge.

Once known as the 'pearl of the Congo' the city could not even boast of any half-decent hotels with air conditioning and Marcel Valerie had to walk half a mile from the muggy Patricio Lumumba avenue before he found the offices belonging to the owner of an important mine.

He had expected to meet with a snappy executive, the man who had promised to provide him with the most lucrative bit of business the new century had seen, but instead he met with a fat, dirty, sour-faced man, who stank of vodka and spoke with a Russian lilt, despite the fact that he was supposedly from Kazakhstan.

"As I already said on the phone," was the first thing that the Kazak said, "I'm not that interested in selling my deposit, but it all comes down to money. I've been in this shit hole for too long. I'm being killed by malaria, and if what you offer me means I can get on with my life again, then maybe we could come to an arrangement."

"As you must understand, I need to visit the mine and the factory first in order to make an evaluation," the visitor said.

"Of course," the large man conceded, "But I'm warning you that what you'll see isn't what the rest of the civilised world would think of as a "factory" or a "mine", which, when all is said and done isn't actually that important. What is important is that we extract the best mineral in the market, that's what matters..." he winked at him in a knowing way before adding, "Wouldn't you agree?"

"Quite so!" the man said. He had travelled a long way and was starting to feel quite tired. "But it is equally important for me to know how it is being produced, how much and for 'how long' it will be producing."

"That's another story my friend!" he exclaimed with a loud guffaw, "And an entirely different thing. This blessed mineral is as capricious as a beautiful woman with whom everybody claims to have slept with; it appears when you were least expecting it to and disappears as suddenly, just when you really want it. A deposit could be making a fortune today and carry you to ruin a week later. That is my risk."

He poured himself a more than generous glass of vodka, without making the slightest move to invite his guest to have one, then added emphatically, "And yours is whether you decide to go with the business or not."

"Can I see what it actually is?"

"That's why you're here isn't it?"

The Kazak took him through a labyrinth of dark alleyways until they reached an enormous shed with a zinc roof that looked more like an oven than a factory, inside of which were about fifty half-naked Congolese men covered in powder from head to toe, all working in time, sieving large quantities of soil that arrived on a conveyor belt in front of them, using only their hands to search for what looked like small greyish, blue stones which they then threw into a chipped container.

The place might have been the waiting room to hell. The air was heavy with the muggy heat and the dust made it hard to

27

breathe, while the smell of sweat and urine permeated the room.

"Jesus Christ!"

"You were warned. This is something that you've probably never seen before, but I give you my word that it is the only way to do it with this elusive son of a bitch that never appears in the veins but is scattered through the soil, all mixed up with bits of wolfram and cassiterite."

The Belgian pointed to the men working in the inhumane conditions.

"How much do they charge?" he asked.

"One euro."

"An hour?"

"Are you mad! A day."

It was mid-afternoon by the time they had gone around the lake and travelled some thirty kilometres aboard a rickety old lorry that seemed to resolutely search out every one of the numerous potholes along the narrow path of red earth that they were driving along. The path wound through gigantic trees and dense lianas until, after sluicing through a small river, they finally arrived at a large clearing where the trees had been ripped out by their roots with dynamite.

Nearly all of the "miners" were boys, many of them still children, and they were crawling on all fours into narrow holes that had been cut in to the banks of the hills, running the risk of being buried alive by a sudden collapse, given that the precarious galleries had no support mechanisms in place whatsoever.

Covered in dust, starving and with reddened eyes, they looked like an army of ghosts that, for a split second simply stared at the recent arrivals as if they had come from another planet.

Ironically, it was the place itself that seemed to belong to another planet.

"And how much do they charge?" Marcel Valerie asked once again.

"Twenty centavos."

"Twenty centavos of a euro with the risk of dying in there?" he exclaimed.

"Nobody forces them."

"Are you sure?"

"Quite."

"And what's the accident rate?"

"Between five and seven deaths a month on average, but this type of work means they don't have to be buried. When they get trapped in a gallery you can just put a cross on top and they rest in peace."

"Cruel but practical nonetheless," the Belgian said. He then stood and studied the scene closely for some time. After a while he took out a small calculator from the pocket of his shirt, that was already drenched in sweat and tapped into it repeatedly while the Kazak watched on, until finally he said casually, "Thirty million, no discussion."

"Euros?"

"Euros."

"My business is all yours!"

USA

Eladio Medrano had built himself a reputation as one of the best criminal defence lawyers in the United States. Most of his accumulated wealth had come from the defence of Mafiosi and South American drug traffickers, who not only liked the way he had with the judges but also the fact that he spoke good Castillian, which made it a lot easier for them to get straight to the point when delicate issues were being discussed.

His current client Robert Carmona, better known by the telling nickname of "Ball-breaker", famous for castrating his enemies and competitors, had been caught in El Paso and charged with bringing in over two hundred tonnes of cocaine to the country by using the curious method of an old Soviet submarine. The cargo had been shipped from Tampico in Mexico to the Matagorda Island, Texas, where it would have continued its journey by road to Houston, Austin or San Antonio.

Eladio Medrano would at any other time in his life, have been happy to take on such a complex, interesting and lucrative case, especially one like this, which would guarantee him significant benefits even if he only managed to secure unconditional bail for his client. But in the last month, since his disturbing meeting with the Dall&Houston executives, the measure of his priorities had taken a swift about-turn.

The assassination of Richard Marzan and Bem Sandorf, whom he had spent a good many hours with, either thrashing out issues around the table in the meeting room or chasing a ball on the lawns of the Pine Crest Golf Club, which he could see from his office windows, had opened his eyes to the painful reality that what now lay at stake was much more than just how much he planned to bill for his next case. What he now faced was the possibility that at any given moment he might end up in a vat of wine, a ceramic pot or indeed any other type of receptacle.

He had spent three days mulling over whether or not to carry on with Carmona's defence or to go in to hiding. But he knew that if he decided to leave this dodgy Mexican in the lurch, then before long one of his henchmen would pay him a visit and in honour of his nickname make mincemeat of his balls.

South American drug traffickers were notoriously unforgiving towards anyone that failed to comply with their wishes.

Mind you, the so-called "Al Rashid" might be equally unforgiving, or worse even.

If only he had not got involved in the stupid plan that ended up with the start of that disastrous war.

He had earned millions from it, but it had also caused him a lot of grief and cost him some friendships, including the respect and love of his eldest daughter whose boyfriend, a Blackwater mercenary, had been beaten to death in a street in Baghdad by an angry mob, his body set alight and hung from a street lamp.

Eladio Medrano was smart enough to realise that he had made a huge mistake, the worst of it being that he had never needed to get involved in the first place.

He had never needed that much money.

The truth was that he had no idea what to do with it all either.

It had become a figure in a current bank account that he hardly touched and more often than not he was completely unaware of how much he had in there anyway.

To have for the sake of having.

To have more for the sake of having more.

They were not gold coins to jingle or sleek bank notes to slip into a wallet; they were just numbers; signs that would never help him make a birdie on the twelfth, an achievement that really would have made him happy, given that it was something he had been trying to do for the last twenty years.

He had not played for two weeks for fear of having his head blown off. Houston's Pine Crest Golf Course was bang in the centre of the city and a good sniper could fire a shot comfortably from any one of the highways surrounding it, that were at most only some four hundred meters away. Over and over again he asked himself what on earth was the point of having all that money when he could not even enjoy his favourite past time.

All he had used it for lately was to buy himself a blacked out car and to pay for half a dozen miserable bodyguards that the tedious Jeff Hamilton had forced on him and who even went with him to the bathroom.

He would have given all of his shares to Hamilton in good faith in exchange for being able to move around freely, but Peter Corkenham had warned them in no uncertain terms that "the rats that tried to abandon the ship right now would pay the consequences immediately."

It was also well known that this son of a whore never made an empty threat. They had all set out together on a risky adventure and he demanded that they continued on it together to the end, come what may.

Every time he got out from the safety of his car and crossed onto the pavement he felt like a sitting duck, despite being surrounded by four enormous "gorillas".

The Palace of Justice was one of the few places where he felt safe, its security service renowned for being one of the most efficient in the country.

Once inside he tried to shrug off his worries and concentrate on the task in hand: to prove that Roberto Carmona had been the victim of corrupt Mexican police dealings and that he had nothing to do with the ancient and rusty Russian submarine that had had the bad luck to run aground on a bank of sand on the Texan coastline, stacked to the ceiling with cocaine.

He found nothing unusual in the fact that his client wanted to see him alone in the small room, where they normally waited until a hearing started, since the savvy Mexican usually had something up his sleeve that would help him slip through the fingers of the law once again.

"So, what's this all about?" he asked.

The well-built man, who was as tall as him but younger and much stronger, looked around as if trying to make sure that there were no hidden microphones or cameras, and then gestured to the lawyer to sit down next to him.

"I have good news..." he murmured in a voice so low that Eladio Medrano had no other option but to move his head closer.

"What did you say?" he asked in the same tone.

The Mexican almost brushed his ear with his mouth as he reiterated in barely a whisper:

"That I have some good news. Yesterday my wife got a visit from someone calling on behalf of a man called something like "Arahum Al Rashid"..."

As he muttered those words he squeezed the lawyer's jaw unusually hard, forcing his mouth to open, then pushed in a small capsule, pushing it to the bottom of his throat and closed it violently so that there was not enough time for him to spit it out, saying:

"He promised me that if I made you swallow this medicine that he'd get me out of here..."

Eladio Medrano tried to free himself of the fierce bear-like grip that held him down, spitting, shouting and struggling, but within seconds he had started to foam at the mouth and convulse violently like a fish out of water.

He fell to the floor kicking and scratching at the walls, screaming in agony while his aggressor got up and started to bang on the door, shouting at the top of his voice:

"Get a doctor, a doctor! The lawyer has had an attack! Get a doctor!"

The scene that followed was one of the most chaotic the Palace of Justice had ever seen, with doctors, nurses and police running from one end of the building to the next, while a well-built man suffering from violent convulsions was carried out on a stretcher and into an ambulance, which left speeding for hospital.

When a bailiff finally remembered to tell "Ball-breaker" that his hearing would obviously be postponed, he was nowhere to be seen.

The only thing that remained in the small room was the body of Eladio Medrano.

Habana, 1947

Mauro Rivero came to the conclusion at a very early age that he was much more intelligent than everybody else around him.

In spite of being a bit of an egomaniac, it was not his egomania that had led him to this conclusion, but simple deduction, as it dawned on him that not one of his teachers appeared able to follow his train of thought.

He also discovered something else that he considered to be of singular importance: that he did not know one single person who did not have a vice that in one way or another limited his or her faculties: drinking, drugs, gambling, sex, an overwhelming greed or the desire for power, which all too often blinded people. He had never experienced the slightest interest in any of those vices, which, without doubt gave him quite an advantage over the rest of the human race.

Mauro did not drink, smoke, take drugs, he felt nothing in the presence of an attractive woman or man, he did not yearn for any type of power, and money was only of interest to him as a means to an end.

He was, however, an extraordinarily good poker player, so ice cold was the blood that ran through his veins and so impassive was he by nature, that his face bore the same expression from the moment he picked up his hand of cards to the moment he got up to leave.

He never turned a game down, but not because it was something he enjoyed, but simply because he saw it as an important exercise in self-control.

Mauro Rivero imagined himself to be a lizard, and occasionally he would lose the game on purpose with the aim of further strengthening his character and training it to accept, from one day to the next, both victory and defeat with total indifference.

"Hammer, anvil, hammer, anvil".

That old-fashioned saying that he had heard since he was a child and that without him really understanding why, always brought fascist images to mind, stayed with him throughout his puberty and seemed to echo of a future where he would not only be dealing out the blows but receiving them too.

All of these thoughts he protected under a mantel of total and absolute indifference because the thing he strived for above all else, was to avoid revealing any kind of sentimentality or weakness, and whether that constituted a huge defect, a foul sin or a worthy virtue, was of little or no concern to him.

He was ashamed of the limitations that this absurd and unknown illness had imposed on him from birth and which he had to live with day in and day out and that may in fact have been the real reason behind why he spent the rest of his life trying to conceal from the world what was happening to his body and mind.

At sixteen years of age he was already the brains behind a network of gangs that had started to take over the streets of Old Havana and at seventeen years of age he started up a lucrative variant on the traditional game of "La Bolita", and before he had even reached adulthood he had founded the already feared and reviled "Corporation", a secret society that soon become synonymous with all things related to vice or corruption in most of Havana's neighbourhoods.

Emiliano Césepedes, his childhood friend, was in charge of the business of prostitution, Bruno "The Knave" with the game, a variant of "La Bolita", Pepe "the Destitute" with keeping in favour with the police, some of whom became his confidants, Nick Kanakis with extortion, Ceferino "The Boner" with drugs, and the blind Baldomero Carreño with "administration".

Too intelligent to call himself "chief", Mauro Rivero gave himself the title of "coordinator" and a smaller salary than his companions since he had no need for money, living in his mother's house and with no vices to speak of.

Still, it was quite clear to everyone involved, from the low class prostitute to the money-grabbing lottery ticket vendor, that he was the one in charge.

Thanks to the power of his information sources, his intelligence and a certain sixth sense he possessed that meant he could sniff out any trouble well before it happened, he was one of the first to work out that the rebel faction that occupied the Sierra Maestra under the leadership of a man called Fidel Castro was planting the seeds of a revolution, that sooner or later would do away with the brutal dictator and corrupt sergeant, self-promoted to the status of "General" Fulgencio Batista.

He also knew that a place where a revolution lay waiting in the wings was no place for the "Corporation" to continue with its underground dealings, especially since it was well-known that his followers had been collaborating quite openly with the Batista regime.

So in October 1959 he suggested to his mother that she take a long break in the Dominican Republic. In November he told his accomplices that it was time they started to look for a future elsewhere if they wanted to avoid the firing squads, and in December he took one last look at the house where he had spent all of his life, filled three bags with documents, including his mother's beauty recipes and got on a boat destined for Miami.

Colorado

The old lady, true to her word, arrived the following afternoon driving a trailer which had everything you could possibly think of packed into it and they took off together, ambling gently through the back roads chatting together for hours in a light-hearted way.

Only later that afternoon and after they had eaten, at the edge of the wood where there was a path that led to a river "full of trout as big as seals", did the old lady finally sit down and ask her on a more serious note:

"So my dear, if we are to go on from here you must tell me who you really are, since I am of the impression that you are no more English than I am Korean."

"My name is Salka Embarek, I am Iraqi and my family died during the bombing of Iraq and I came into this country illegally, so that if the police catch me, I will be accused of being a terrorist and spend the rest of my life in prison."

"Right! If you are Iraqi and they killed your family, nothing else matters. We won't mention it again."

The young girl was dumbstruck and her mouth fell open in disbelief as she stuttered:

"What do you mean we won't discuss it again? I've just told you that I could be accused of terrorism and the police are looking for me and you are so calm. I can't believe it!"

"The police have a habit of picking on the wretched and ignoring the ones that are really doing the damage, which is usually the politicians that are paying them their salaries," she replied calmly. "Whatever crime you have committed, if any, even the worst one would not compare with those committed by today's governments who are responsible for this cruel, bloody and unjust war in your country," she said and then smiling broadly, she added, "But who am I to judge you. The past is the past. What matters now is the future. What plans do you have?"

"None."

"Sure?"

"Sure. I came here to kill Americans but I have come to realise that revenge serves nobody."

"I wouldn't know my dear. As far as I remember I haven't had any reason to seek revenge on anyone."

"Lucky you! While I was waiting at the hotel I saw on television that five hundred people in Iraq died in three separate incidents yesterday, by car bombs and lorries filled with petrol. This war started four years ago and every day things are getting worse. What will become of this country where I was born?"

"A tricky question my dear. Very tricky. These days it's much cheaper to destroy than to rebuild, making the foundations upon which our society is built more fragile by the day. Something is wrong when it's the people that manufacture bombs and missiles, capable of wiping out an entire city, that make more money than the people producing the very materials we use to build them with. It is without doubt a very perplexing and curious phenomenon. At least it is to me."

She threw up her hands in an exasperated gesture, adding, "But we should let this alone right now since the solution is clearly out of our hands. What would you like to do now?"

"I've already said, I don't know."

"No my girl," she exclaimed, "You told me you didn't know what you were going to do now, not what would you would *like* to do now. These are two different things altogether."

"It isn't actually that different. It was only the other day I was planning on blowing myself up. Anyway, my passport is false, so even if I do look for work they'll discover who I am and lock me up."

"Don't worry about that," came her immediate reply, "This country is so vast, complex and wild that I've known surgeons who've worked without ever having been to university and judges that have never qualified as lawyers. There was an unusual case just recently when a teacher was found to have been working in a school for twenty years without knowing how to read and was apparently in denial of the very fact herself," she said, adding, "Here you can be sentenced to death for a crime in one state but if you cross that invisible line you become subject to another set of rules that may or may not be more permissive; on the East Coast it might mean one thing and on the West another. What is important is that you know the tricks and who to turn to."

"And do you know whom to turn to?"

"Remember the saying: "better the devil you know than the devil you don't", oh and this devil's a female by the way."

"Maybe you don't mind being associated with me then?"

"Maybe I look like a terrorist?"

"Maybe I don't. Apparently we're supposed to try and look as defenceless and inoffensive as possible and anyway no one actually looks like a terrorist apart from the characters you see in those action films about terrorists."

"You've got a point."

"Yes, I do. The people that recruited me looked like carpet salesman and that was because in reality they were carpet salesmen. They lightened my hair, gave me an intensive course on life in England and how to come across as being younger and more stupid than I am, and then they brought me here, supposedly to kill Americans."

"But you haven't killed anyone yet?" she said and smiling broadly again, she added, "That is all I need to know. Now then, do you know how to play cards?"

Paris 2007

Marcel Valerie waited until the waiters had poured the coffee and withdrawn discreetly, leaving them alone at the elegant table he had reserved, before launching into the meeting. It was the kind of table that hundreds of multimillionaires had sat at before them to clinch many a high-end business deal or negotiate delicate political treaties.

The Belgian quickly finished his coffee and smiling, almost coyly, he asked:

"How much are you buying it for?"

"Three thousand five hundred a kilo."

"How much is it producing?"

"About one hundred tons of unrefined material a year."

"Is that enough for you?"

"I have no choice. The material is harder to come by and the market is more tricky by the minute."

"But what do you really need?" Marcel Valerie asked pointedly, "What would you be happy with?"

"Happy?" his companion said, a little confused now, "I would be happy getting as much as I could get my hands on, but it would have to be a guaranteed amount because I can't increase production, then spend a fortune on machinery only to find that I'm short of the primary material."

"Would you invest this 'fortune' if I guaranteed you three hundred tons a year over a period of five years?"

"Of course! Although that would still depend on the price..." he said, wagging his finger.

"Half of what you're paying now."

The other man stared in disbelief before asking, "What did you say?"

"I said that it would cost you half of what you're paying right now."

"Are you playing games with me?"

The Belgian took a while to answer, sipping his cognac slowly, conscious of the fact that his offer had made quite an impression. Finally and with a slight curl of his lips he asked, "Have I ever played games with you before when we've done business? As far as I remember we signed our first bit of business about fifteen years ago and you've never had any reason to complain."

"That's very true, but what you're proposing to me today..."

"What I am offering you today will make me a lot of money as long as you can guarantee me that you won't renege upon this deal and that you'll pay me for three hundred tons a year over a period of five years at one thousand, seven hundred and fifty euros a kilo."

"When and where shall I sign?"

The Belgian bent down and picked up his briefcase then opened it up to reveal a pile of documents.

"Here. And now," he said. "This is a pre-contract that you can look over in more detail with your lawyers. Your signature is all I need now."

"Thank you for your confidence. But are you sure you know what you are doing?"

"Absolutely."

"You can guarantee me three hundred tons at this price for that amount of time?" he repeated again, as if he was still unable to believe that such a deal existed.

"With a penalty of four million if I fail to deliver for fifteen days after the due date. But be warned, that same penalty applies to you if you fail to pay me."

"If it's good material then there is no reason why I wouldn't pay you for it."

"Its purity is guaranteed at 93%."

"That's not possible!" Raymond Barriere exclaimed, even more confused than ever. "It's not possible! No one in their right mind would offer a similar deal without going under."

42

"My judgment is in no way impaired, my friend, and I don't have any intention of ruining myself. When you shoot yourself in the head it's a messy business and you don't look so good in photos anymore..." he held out a gold pen and with a slightly mocking smile asked, "Will you sign or not? If you don't do it Ericsson, Nokia, IBM, Motorola, or Siemens will... I offered you first pick because we go back a long way, but you know as well as I do that once I put this deal out there, it won't so much as touch the ground."

"I'm sure of that," the white-haired man mumbled. "As sure as I am that you're a damn trouble-maker and that you must know something I don't," he said looking at him inquisitively, then he asked, "Tell me the truth. Do you know something I don't?"

"Of course I do my friend. Naturally!" he admitted unashamedly. "It would be silly to deny it. Privileged information is the basis of most business deals these days, and since you know me, you know very well that I always have the best information at my fingertips."

He held the pen between his fingers and tapped the back of his hand affectionately. "What I can assure you is that you will not regret signing here. You're making one of the best deals of your life."

Barriere began to sign where the other man indicated he should do so, whilst muttering:

"I think I'm already starting to regret this."

Miami, 1961

Before the year was even up, Mauro Rivero realized that the "Corporation", which had worked so effectively in La Havana could work just as well in Miami, since the place was overrun with Cuban exiles, so long as long as they had figured out how to adapt to the new country and its customs.

"Vices are vices and the language they speak are one and the same anywhere," he would say, convinced that gambling, alcohol, prostitution, drugs and bribery worked in the same way on both sides of the wide ocean that separated the Cuban island from the Florida peninsula.

So he began the arduous task of finding and reorganizing his team, which he managed to do with the exception of the shy and retiring Baldomero Carreño, who had made the mistake of running into the streets, drunk on patriotic sentiment, shouting "Long live the revolution! Long live Fidel!" Not long after that, having been denounced by a spiteful neighbour, he found himself, in the name of the revolution, doing eight years hard labour for being a pimp, when all he had ever really done was to administrate, very efficiently, a handful of brothels that were legal under the island's prevailing laws at that time.

Fidel Castro rose to power on the promise that Cuba would no longer be North America's luxury brothel and he achieved it. In a few years it became the cheapest brothel in the world, a fact that did not, however, appease Carreño whose life had indeed been ruined by it.

Nonetheless, business in Miami flourished in solid dollars as opposed to a fluctuating peso, thanks to the large amount of beautiful mixed-race women, who having managed to escape the communist regime, had become objects of great demand for the crowds of fair-haired tourists that arrived in Miami daily. That and income from the clandestine game of Bolita, which provided some of the exiles with the only hope of ever escaping the miserable situation they found themselves in, having been forced to abandon their homes in Cuba with nothing more than the clothes on their backs.

Mauro Rivero soon learnt a basic rule that he made his people follow to the letter: in the United States the hand of justice can be avoided as long as you did not get mixed up in drug trafficking or kidnapping.

Any other type of crime could be sorted out, more often than not, with money and a good lawyer.

He also learnt one other golden rule: that in 'Little Havana' nothing was as it seemed and of all the political refugees that claimed to be staunch enemies of the communist regime, at least one in every fifty was actually a spy in Castro's service.

He therefore forced himself to maintain completely neutral relationships with all of his associates, which was never that hard for someone as indifferent as he was.

He worked with both pro and anti Castro types, without giving their political leanings a second thought, since he did not have a political bone in his body.

His one priority remained the same; to never get cold and on that level Miami was the ideal place for him.

Everything was going smoothly and to plan, with the large amounts of money pouring in being hidden successfully behind the cover of his cosmetics company, that he had built using his mother's very own recipes, until one ill-fated day when the press seized upon the story of a young black boy, a child, found dead on the beach, his body displaying clear signs of having been violently and cruelly tortured.

It was not the first time that something like this had happened in Florida, but to Mauro Rivero the modus operandi was identical to the case of three children that had been found violated and assassinated in La Havana some years before. After putting two and two together, followed by a round of discreet enquiries, he arrived at the painful conclusion that the person he had suspected while he was still in Cuba, and who was responsible for this latest lewd affair, was none other than his associate and co-founder of the "Corporation", the nasty Ceferino 'The Boner'.

He paced up and down the beach in search of a solution, fully aware that if he went to the police he ran the risk of being exposed during the investigation as this degenerate son of a bitch's partner in the "Corporation".

So he decided on another equally effective solution to the problem by paying a visit to his chiropodist Javier Velásquez, to see if he might be able to relieve him of this enormous callous that was annoying him to the point of distraction.

After studying his feet for some while, the slightly disconcerted "Negro Velásquez" lifted his head up, surprised by the perfection of his delicate and immaculate feet and asked sarcastically, "Where exactly is this calloused lump, brother?"

"He's very tall, mixed race, bald and always wears dark glasses. He lunches every day in the Rufino Tavern very near to Hotel Clay on Miami Beach."

"Shed some light brother on the situation, my speciality is feet, remember."

"Do you remember the case of the three boys that were violated, tortured and assassinated in La Havana some years ago?"

"I remember. You don't forget something that horrific in a hurry."

"What do you think Fidel's police would do if they knew that the degenerate responsible for those killings was running around free in Miami, doing the same things?"

"They would take it very badly."

"And you would take care of the problem quietly and once and for all, wouldn't you?"

"Of course brother, since Fidel has very little jurisdiction in

Miami and those gringos will dig out someone to blame, whether they were guilty or not."

"I'm very happy to hear it. How much do I owe you for the consultation?"

"The first one is free."

"Thank you and good day!"

"Good day."

Two weeks later, Ceferíno "The boner" was shot down by four bullets as he walked out of a discothèque on Miami Beach, not far from Hotel Clay.

Rumours soon spread that Fidel Castro had sent in someone to assassinate a very dangerous political enemy.

"Seven Oaks" Texas, 2007

Peter Corkenham sounded quite sincere when he greeted his guest:

"Thank you for coming."

"No problem."

"Well, actually there is a problem. I know that you told us a while back and in no uncertain terms that you wanted nothing more to do with us. Well, we have a problem and I need you now, more than I ever have done."

Tony Walker observed the president of Dall&Houston, who in turn watched him with a slightly mocking smile playing at his lips, then shrugged his shoulders.

"I don't think I can be of much help here…" he said. "What do you want from me?"

"I'm not exactly sure, but I suppose you've heard of this son of a bitch that calls himself "Al Rashid" who has already finished off three of our board members. The problem here is that we are businessmen not action men. You're the only one I know who has experience in this line of work."

"Experience?" his guest said in a horrified tone, "What on earth are you referring to, Peter? Nobody has experience with a madman that says build hospitals and schools or fifteen people die. This has never happened before."

"This is true."

"So?"

"I believe you have good contacts."

"How could I possibly have better contacts than you? It's well known that you meet with "Iceman" every Wednesday and it can only be presumed that as vice-president you have the FBI the CIA and all the police units in the country, including the famous Blackwater lot at your service. What can I possibly do that they can't?"

"That may be so," Peter Corkenham said casually, "But all I know is that the mercenaries that Hamilton hired for the price of gold, don't seem to be able to stop the killings. The way they got rid of Medrano was a true work of art."

"It may have been mere coincidence; maybe he just paid the price for trying to get Carmona off the hook."

"I don't believe in coincidences, especially when my own neck is on the block. "Al Rashid" is very clever man, which is why we need someone cleverer than him."

"I guess you're referring to Mariel."

"Exactly."

"I believe he's retired."

"He has to come back."

"What?"

"Offer him what he wants," he replied firmly. "You are the only one that knows how to find him and I assure you that if I have to choose between my life, paying one billion dollars or signing a nine-figure cheque to Mariel, I'd rather choose the last one."

"What do you think he can do about it?"

"I haven't got the vaguest idea, but someone who has managed a criminal organisation for half a century with such incredible efficiency that no-one ever has ever found out who is behind it, means a lot more to me than that bunch of cretins at the FBI or the CIA who weren't even smart enough to notice that a dozen fanatics were training at their very own flying schools right under their noses, with a plot to hijack four planes and drive them in to the Twin Towers. They haven't even managed to catch that evasive Osama Bin Laden, who's been running a merry circle around them ever since."

"Iceman wouldn't like to hear you say that."

"I bet that underneath it all he'd agree with me, but I don't want to waste time deliberating on what a politician might really think, especially him," Peter Corkenham said closing the subject.

"With the sword of Damocles hanging over my head and the rest of my main collaborators, I cannot work in peace."

He paused for a while looking across at his acquaintance as if trying to assess whether or not to confide in him, before finally enquiring, "What do you know about coltan?"

"About what?"

"About a mineral called coltan."

"Very little to be honest. Not much at all."

"I thought as much. Nobody seems to know anything about it, so before going ahead with this I'd like you to take a look at this report. I'm going for a horse ride and after supper I'll tell you in more detail what this is all about."

He put a file on the table, gave his guest a few encouraging slaps on the back and left the room.

Tony Walker remained there, somewhat perplexed at how their conversation had taken such a sharp and unexpected turn. Through the large windows he watched his host leave the porch, mount a beautiful black mare and charge out in to the fields, accompanied by his inseparable friend Jeff Hamilton and followed by half a dozen heavily armed bodyguards.

It was obvious that the president of Dall&Houston was running scared, even within the confines of his own ranch. Only once they had disappeared behind a cloud of dust kicked up by the horses, did he settle down to look at the document, the first page of which had printed on it just the one word:

"COLTAN"

Coltan is an abbreviation of columbite-tantalite, a set of minerals that form when they are fused together. It is a dull metallic blue colour and tantalum is extracted from it. Tantalum has a very high resistance to heat as well as possessing other extraordinary electrical properties.

Australia is the main producer, while there are proven

reserves and or exploitation of them in Brazil, Thailand and the Democratic Republic of Congo, this last holds some 80% of the world's estimated reserves. According to reports from international agencies and the press, coltan exports have helped to finance the various groups involved in the 'Second Congo War', a conflict that has so far led to the deaths of some four million people. Rwanda and Uganda currently export stolen coltan to the United States where it is being used in the fabrication of elements of high technology like mobile phones, DVD scanners, video game consoles etc...

Columbite and tantalite are considered highly strategic metals and the fact that 80% of reserves are to be found in the Democratic republic of Congo, would explain why this country has been at war since 1998, why its neighbours Rwanda and Uganda have a military presence in part of the Congolese territory and why four million people have died since the start of this war. Coltan is essential for the development of new technologies, space stations, and space travel and above all for use in the manufacture of guided weapons

It is not necessary to be an authority on international law to realise that this war constitutes one of the greatest injustices, on a global scale, ever to have been committed against a sovereign State. In the last few decades we have seen many a country come under siege, including the military occupation of independent countries: Iraq invaded Kuwait and the United States did the same in Granada, although with different results. Countries like Afghanistan and Iraq have been bombed, with only marginal protection coming from the UN. The anomaly lies in the case above however, where occupation of a territory is based simply upon the exploitation of its mineral resources, while its population is systematically annihilated. This type of aggression has not been committed since the invasion of the European countries by Germany's Hitler .

According to a group of United Nations experts, the Patriotic Rwandan Party has set up a unit in order to oversee mineral activity in the Congo and establish contacts with western companies and clients. The mineral is transported in lorries to Kigali, the capital of Rwanda where it is treated in plants owned by the Rwanda Mining Society, before being exported. The mineral ends up in the Unites States, Germany, Holland, Belgium and Kazakhstan.

The Big Lake Mining Society has a monopoly on the sector and finances the rebel movement "Congolese Regrouping for Democracy" which has about 40,000 soldiers and is backed by Rwanda.

They earn 200,000 dollars a month from diamond sales, while sales of coltan bring in well over a million.

Information available, privy to the United Nations, reveals that the trafficking is organised by the daughter of the Kazakh president Nursultan Nazarbaev who is married to the director general of a Kazakh company that extracts uranium, coltan and other strategic minerals.

This, by and large, is the spider's web of international business that is feeding a war in the heart of Africa that watches on as its own citizens become more impoverished by the day, despite it being one of the richest countries on earth. There is more: the Information Service for International peace has carried out a detailed study of those western companies that are currently dealing in coltan and therefore financing the war in the Democratic Republic of Congo.

Alcatel, Compaq, Dell, Ericsson, HP, IBM, Lucent, Motorola, Nokia, Siemens and other leading companies all use condensers and other components that contain tantalum; the companies that make these components like *AMD, AVX, Epcos, Hitachi, Intel, Kemet, NEC,* also use it.

It must be reiterated that these dealings are guilty of fuelling a war that although seemingly forgotten is in no way any less dramatic. A further aggravating factor: it is feared that this very same territory in the Democratic Republic of Congo is under threat of being broken up. That is to say, divided in to various states in order to facilitate the exploitation of its resources.

These were the very fears expressed by the late archbishop of Bukavu, Monseñor Christophe Munzihirwa, who was assassinated by the Rwandan army.

The Centre for International Studies of Tantalum and Niobium in Belgium (one of the countries that has traditionally been linked to the Congo), has recommended to international buyers that they avoid purchasing coltan from the Congo for ethical reasons. From an economic standpoint there are some multinational companies and large buyers that remain unconcerned by the social conflict that lies behind the extraction of this mineral and do not want the awful truth behind it to be made public by the media. The media are by the same token somewhat conditioned by the fear that they could also lose an important part of their advertising income, were they to run an exposé.

The "magical" physical-chemical properties of this mineral mean that it is indispensable to the electronic apparatus industry, nuclear and space centres, industries of non-invasive apparatus used in medical diagnosis, magnetic trains, fibre optics etc...

However, 60% of production is used in the elaboration of condensers and other mobile phone parts. The big brands are starting to hustle for control of the region using their indigenous contacts in a phenomenon that Madeleine Albright has called the "first African world war". In 1997 the Congolese president Mobutu Sese Seko, distantly related to some important French imperialists, was overthrown. Kagame, the current president of Rwanda, who studied at military centres in the European Union and England and Museveni, president of Uganda, a country that Washington holds up as an example to the African nations, led the take-over of the DRC capital, Kinshasa and put the country under the control of their friend Laurent Kabila.

Mining concessions were then distributed between various companies, including Canada's Barrick Gold Corporation, America Mineral Fields, in which Bush, father of the current president of the United States, has notable interests.

Colorado, 2007

The trout were indeed like seals. They took the bait readily and were easily caught by the two women, one older, the other barely a girl, both of whom were having the holiday of a lifetime in a calm corner of paradise.

Their friendship had started to take form some two weeks beforehand and was cemented during those days by the river, despite the fact that there was an age gap of fifty years between them. Maybe it was not just the case of a simple friendship starting up, but more the fact that both of them had found somebody in whom they could confide and lean on.

Shy, abused, bitter or solitary people often have huge reserves of unused love hiding in the shadows, waiting to be unleashed and often have a more urgent need than most to channel this energy into somewhere or to someone.

They talked nineteen to the dozen as they fished, from dawn to sunset and after supper over lengthy card games that only ever ended because they no longer had the energy to hold the cards up in their weary hands.

From time to time they went into the local village to buy provisions, but otherwise they remained hidden away from all human contact, from a world they did not care to be part of.

Their world became the woods that surrounded them, the running river, the smells of a thousand different flowers, the bird songs and the splashing trout.

One afternoon a wild boar appeared out of nowhere and started sniffing around, so the old woman pulled out a gun from her jacket pocket, something she always carried with her, come rain or shine, and shot the boar in the head. That evening they roasted the hog slowly over a beautiful fire and had something of a party.

At the end of the night, their spirits high on a few glasses of

Californian wine, Mary Lacombe said casually, "I've given your situation and how you might escape the police a lot of thought."

"And?"

"I've decided that the best way would be for me to adopt you."

The girl stared at her in disbelief.

"What did you say?" she almost stuttered.

"I said I could adopt you, but backdate the papers."

"What on earth do you mean?"

"I know people that can fiddle the papers to say that you were born in some back of beyond South American country then raised in England and I adopted you as a child, so that there is no way you could be suspected of being an Iraqi terrorist."

"Can you really pull that off?" The oung woman was astounded.

"You can do anything you want in this country with a bit of money."

"I guess it would cost a lot of money."

"That is of no consequence, little one. I've still got some savings that my late husband left me."

"I wouldn't let you use up your savings that you might need one day, on adopting me," she shook her head firmly. "I am so grateful for these few days of peace that you have already given me, days that will help me face up to what life throws at me from here on. I'm just grateful you haven't turned me in..." her voice trailed off.

"I don't see it like that and I think that in this instance my opinion counts too," said Mary firmly.

"You don't see it like that because you're too generous, but I don't have the right to mess up a peaceful and calm life like yours with my problems that have nothing to do with you."

"How can you say that you have "nothing to do with me"? You are the only person I've ever really spent any time with in recent years?" she replied, growing annoyed now with the girl's refusal. "Who do you want me to worry about? My greengrocer who's a sour-faced drunk or my hairdresser that talks so much rubbish he actually gives me a headache as he sets my hair for me."

"For your parents, even though they are far away."

"I don't have any parents near or far. Apart from the fact that friendship is much stronger than any parental relationship since it isn't the result of blood ties but straightforward sentiment. Quite often a friend is more important than a sibling, and you know it."

"My parents and siblings meant everything to me."

"Because you lost them when you very young, and maybe only because of that my dear," she said wisely. "If they hadn't gone so suddenly you would have forged your own path away from them, in time. That isn't to say that you would ever have stopped loving them, just that your priorities would have changed with a husband and your own children." She reached out and stroked the girl's hand affectionately.

"You are my priority and I would like to know that I am yours, because right now we only have each other."

Texas, 2007

Until now there have been two factions, neither of which have ever been that clearly defined, fighting the war. Rwanda, Uganda and Burundi, backed by the EU, financed by credit from the IMF and World Bank and on the other side Angola, Namibia, Zimbabwe and Chad and the Hutu and Maji-Maji militias. In 1999 the opposing factions agreed on a division of territory in the Lusaka Accord, a handy distribution of territory reminiscent of the 1885 Berlin Conference, when the European powers divided up the continent in order to make the exploitation and ransacking of it that much easier.

The workforce they use is made up of peasants, refugees, prisoners of war to whom they promise a reduced sentence and thousands of children, whose bodies can slither easily into the mines in the ground. The recruitment of this work force is double-edged, commercial and coercive, in a double-edged work market. The mineral zones and the areas of military operation have become confused. The frequent migration of people from other famine zones is key if a workforce is to be maintained, given that there are so many deaths in the mines. The capitalist set-up also recruits workers from neighbouring countries by force. They are taken hostage by armed gangs, having already abandoned their homes to become miners. These workers recover coltan from dawn to dusk and eat and sleep in the forests of this mountainous region.

"What do you think?"

"Well, if the report's reliable then it's definitely impressive."

"It's reliable to the last word, I'm sure of that," Peter Corkenham said confidently, slowly stirring his coffee. "I didn't want it to be changed or watered down in anyway just so that you could get the most accurate overview of the situation."

"I certainly have that now," Tony Walker felt obliged to admit, "But what I'm not clear on is why all this sudden interest in the finer details of coltan?"

"Because it's about the future. Very soon whoever doesn't have access to coltan will be sidelined from the telecommunications industry, or more importantly the industry of guided weapon production. As a result we have reached the conclusion that this metal should not be allowed to fall into the hands of guerrillas, mercenaries, bandits or governments, organisations built on nepotism, corruption and egoism."

"Knowing you as I do, and knowing the company that you manage, it is fairly clear that you have reached the decision that it is time that the company took control of its production."

"Its production, distribution and sales. As you know the basis of most of our sales comes from oil, but these days oil is split between so many different parties and they're finding new oilfields every day, in the most unsuspecting of places..."

They were sitting on the spacious porch overlooking the Texan prairies under the light of a full moon. The owner of the magnificent and gigantic ranch put his coffee to one side, poured himself a drink and said:

"What a shame you don't drink. It focuses the thoughts."

"It only confuses mine," he said drily.

"After the fourth glass I get confused, which is why I never get to that number..." he made a slight movement as if to toast the health of his companion, sipped it and savoured it for a minute before swallowing. "We have lost control of Venezuela, where Hugo Chávez does whatever takes his fancy, the Iranians are our worst enemies, the Saudis can no longer be deceived and charge a fortune in commission, Iraq needs to recover its production pace, the Russians say they've found incredible reserves under the North Pole, even the Chinese believe they have enough to cover demand with the crude oil reserves they've discovered under the Yellow Sea. Too many dogs and too many bones! It's time to explore new horizons because its obvious that nobody will ever manage to secure a monopoly on the oil industry."

"And have you reached the conclusion that coltan is a much safer and more lucrative business?"

"Of course! A barrel of oil costs seventy dollars and is infinitely harder to transport than a kilo of coltan, which goes at the moment for four thousand dollars and will soon cost ten thousand. As you've seen, most of it is found in the Congo. Whoever controls the Congo, controls the market. That is our objective."

"Ambitious, definitely."

"We'll use what we earned in Iraq which, as I'm sure you understand, will not be going towards the rebuilding of their schools or hospitals. Regarding coltan, the future of our industries is at stake here and I assure you that for our country, even if it means risking our lives, we'll take that risk."

"For Christ's sake Peter!" exclaimed his companion, tapping his forearm affectionately, "Remember that you're talking to me and not the press. These puffed up arguments go without saying. I agree that this could be the start of some the biggest business this centuries' ever seen, but don't try and flog me a donkey covered in stars and stripes. I don't buy donkeys, I sell them."

"Ok, I won't try and flog you the donkey, but do you realise now that the last thing I need is some mad Moor knocking off my people. I need them by me."

"But to start another war? We're still in the throes of one that we can't get out of."

"Defeat isn't always what it seems, Tony. On some occasions a good defeat is better than a bad victory, which damages patriotic pride. You learn from it."

"What have we learned then on this occasion?"

"That we have an army and we gave it everything it needed in order to achieve a rapid and spectacular victory, but we failed to take into account the amount of sacrifice, patience and resistance that an invading force needs to have in an enemy country. In war, as in almost everything, getting to the top is the easy part, it's keeping up there that's difficult."

"So you're saying that in Iraq we didn't lose the war; we lost the peace."

"Exactly! On the day that the statues of Saddam Hussein fell we should have taken to the streets with flags flapping in the wind to the sound of drums and trumpets, but we decided to remain silent and we fucked up."

"Do you remember that the people who tried their hardest to make us stay there were the Dall&Houston shareholders."

"I know. And that's what I mean when I talk about coltan, I don't want to make the same mistake. We have to come up with a strategy that means we can control the deposits in the Congo without getting either our government or the army involved out there."

Miami

"Negro Velásquez" called him up to remind him that the next day he had a follow-up appointment for the corn on his foot. Mauro Rivero, reading between the lines, turned up on time for his appointment, removed his socks and shoes so that he could put his feet in a bowl of warm water and asked, "What's all this nonsense about these supposed corns that I have then, my friend?"

"They want to talk to you, the ones that sorted out your 'Bone' of contention."

"I always thought it was me that sorted out everyone else's problems."

"It's you that keeps everyone guessing, brother. The favour was mutual and I think this is about much the same thing, a mutual favour."

"To be perfectly honest, Negro," Mauro Rivero said with studied calm, "Things are going pretty well for me and I'm not in any great need of favours."

"All the more reason for you to take a look at the offers on the table then. If you don't need it then you can be the one to set the price."

"The correct response, yes sir! Who do I need to see?"

The chiropodist put a piece of paper in his hand saying, "It's all noted down here, in black and white, brother." Then, smiling broadly he added, "As regards the corn, you don't need to come back and see me again."

Two days later, as night was falling, Mauro Rivero waited at the pre-arranged meeting spot until a green van appeared, picked him up and headed off on the highway that led to Tampa.

He was surprised to find that the van was being driven by a woman alone, and after looking at her for some time, he ventured, "I know you; you're one of "Green Papaya's" girls." He searched his memory before adding, "Sandra "Bigmouth", am I right?"

The woman nodded her head without looking at him.

"I can see you've got a good memory, but you've never been one of my clients."

"I was your boss."

"I know. Officially my boss was that mother-fucker Emiliano Céspedes, who as far as I know is still in the same line of work here in Miami, but it was no secret that it was really you that dished out the orders. That's why you're here now."

"Explain yourself, darling."

The ex-employee of La Havana's most famous brothel stopped the van in amongst some trees, switched off the engine and lit a short Havano cigar before turning to look him straight in the eye.

"All right!" she said, "I'll get straight to the point. I am convinced that you are the cleverest, most astute and furtive person that I've ever known, and a lot of people in Cuba think the same, which is why we think it makes more sense to get you on our side than have you operating on the other one."

"And what is your side?"

"You know that well enough. You were the one that went to see "Negro Velásquez" after all."

"You mean you've gone from being a whore to a revolutionary?"

"I was a revolutionary before becoming a whore, or should I say they made me a whore because I was a revolutionary. You might not believe it, but the "Green Papaya" usually has more information on the troop's movements than they do in the Ministry of Defence."

"I can well believe it; almost everything I ever wanted to know I got from your companions at the brothel. What do you want from me?"

"Information. That's your strength isn't it?"

"Possibly. What type of information?"

"Whatever can be of use to us, especially anything to do with the exact time and place of the invasion."

"You're that sure they'll go ahead with another invasion?" Mauro Rivero said, sounding surprised. "The one in the Dominicans was a resounding disaster."

"Leónidas Trujillo is a stupid puppet and his threats are of no concern to us, but in January that pretty boy Kennedy will get in to power and we're convinced that it won't be long before he needs to prove that he isn't just the son of a multimillionaire and that he'll go for us. One of the Batista generals has formed a group called the 'White Rose' that's working with the CIA and recruiting volunteers, mainly mercenaries. We want you to infiltrate and become part of this group."

"I've never been interested in politics."

-I know, but in this case it's not about politics, it's about money," Sandra "Bigmouth" said, exhaling a jet of smoke through the window as she mulled over the issue. "Anyone driven by ideology is dangerous because at any one moment they might change their leaning, but those people motivated purely by money don't tend to change their objective as they know well enough that they could lose the money and their life. We're talking big money for this deal."

"How much?"

"One hundred thousand dollars now, more along the way as you start giving us information that we can verify and one million if you manage to get us the exact date and more importantly the exact spot where they plan to land."

"How long have I got to think about this?"

"As long as it takes us to get back to Miami. But don't forget; if you accept and then betray us, you're a dead man."

"Tell me something I don't know. With so much money at stake blood gets spilled, it's part and parcel..." Mauro Rivero was silent for a while, thinking over the proposal, closely observed by the ex-prostitute who monitored his every move, until finally and after letting out a short sigh he said, "I like the idea and I agree with the price, but there's something that worries me."

"What's that?"

"The timing. If it's only a question of months how am I going to be able to get into the anti-Castro organisations quick enough? Everyone in Miami knows that I've always steered clear of confrontation."

"That's why we've come to you. Nobody will suspect you."

"But they might start to if I suddenly change my attitude," he paused briefly, before saying with some deliberation, "Unless..."

"Unless what?" she butted in.

"Unless, the Castro supporters gave me no choice but to take sides."

"I'm trying to follow you..."

"It's easy. If Fidel Castro messes with me, then it's only logical that I'd try getting my own back, so joining up with the opposition party might be a credible reaction and no one would think twice about it."

"I still think you're the cleverest kid in town so I don't know how on earth we'd be able to screw you over."

"You of all people should know since you're the one in the business of screwing people," Mauro Rivero said with a slight smile. "There are many different ways," he continued with assurance. "For example burning down my house, destroying my cosmetics empire or putting my physical integrity at risk." He smiled mischievously before concluding. "The second point, the business, would be the most efficient, as long as you paid for the damage."

"How much would it cost to destroy the business?"

"About fifty thousand dollars, although we could make out afterwards that it cost way more. Also, since I have no insurance, I would be so utterly enraged that nobody would think twice if the next day I joined up with the 'White Rose' conspirators."

"I like working with you," the girl confessed. "In La Havana I already admired you because you were different to everyone else and even though you tried your hardest to go unnoticed, you somehow towered above everyone else around you."

"Do not idolize me!" he said in a disconcertingly serious tone. "Do not forget that! If we have to work together then you must never idolize me. I don't trust sycophants."

"Admiration has nothing to do with being sycophantic," she said, exhaling smoke.

"That might be, but personally I've never been able to tell the difference."

***

Gus Callow often boasted about how he had caught some of the best flying fish in the Caribbean, and he may well have been right.

His boat the "Barracuda III$^{\circ}$", almost twenty metres in length, was totally rigged up for deep-sea fishing and able to respond with incredible speed to whatever manoeuvre they needed to make once they got a bite, which was why it was strange that on this particularly fine day he had left the marina much later than usual, accompanied by his three sour-faced, heavily armed body guards.

Once on board Gus Callow, would put the business world behind him and start to feel safe from harm once again. With three of his associates on the Dall&Houston board of directors now dead, feeling safe did not register in his world too often these days, as the people Jeff Hamilton had hired to protect them had so far been totally ineffective .

He had been furious then, when the captain of his beloved "Barracuda III^{a}" had phoned him to tell him that there had been a small breakdown in the boat's electrical system, but regained his composure as quickly, once the captain had reassured him that that the technicians would be able to have it sorted out by Friday morning.

Which was why, on that particular Friday, he had gone out four hours later than usual. Once out at sea though, it was not long before his worries melted away and the day started to look promising with his first few catches; a beautiful flying fish and three enormous dorados.

As afternoon fell and he sat comfortably in his armchair, a glass of rum in his hands and a cigar between his teeth, waiting for a fresh bite, the captain received a mysterious phone call.

"If you would be so kind as to look in your cupboard you will see that to your right we have placed a bomb," said a gruff, but calm voice. "Do not touch it or it will blow you pieces."

The poor man, now pale and trembling, did as he had been told and opened the cupboard, only to discover a large packet that had certainly not been there a few days beforehand, at least not before the electricians had been there.

"What do you mean by this?" he stuttered.

"Nothing that you need to worry about," said a voice that was slow and measured.

"How can I not be worried when there's a bomb on board?" he gasped.

"By me reassuring you that, apart from your boss, none of you will come to any harm. By dialling a telephone number right now I can activate the bomb and the boat will be decimated into splinters, but if you do as I say, I will deactivate it by making another call."

"What do I have to do?"

"Throw Gus Callow overboard."

"What did you say?" he stuttered, thinking that he must have misheard.

"You heard. If you throw your boss overboard and leave him to fend for himself in the open sea, I will deactivate the bomb."

"Are you mad?" the miserable captain said falteringly,

completely dumbfounded.

"Yes!" said the voice on the line. "Your boss and his associates are behind the deaths of almost half a million civilians and four thousand American soldiers, which means that's thirty thousand a head. He deserves to end up at the bottom of the sea and there's no reason why you or anyone else on board should pay for a crime that you haven't committed, although I can guarantee you that very soon I may have to take steps in that direction. Think about your wife, your daughters and the men who you are responsible for at this moment."

"But I'm not a murderer."

"I'm sure you're not, but one of Callow's bodyguards is. Explain the situation to them and let them decide."

"Jesus Christ! This is a nightmare!"

"That pig's created a living nightmare for millions of innocent people. And stop rubbing your eyes. They'll fall out."

The captain, even more disconcerted than ever now, stopped what he was doing and stood there stupefied before asking, "Can you see me?"

"I can see everything going on your boat; even how you boss is trying to light up his cigar again in the wind. My people managed to put up some mini cameras that send me images via your satellite dish."

"I don't believe it!"

"Well please do, because I'm not playing funny games. Enough talk! You make a decision or in ten minutes you'll find yourself at the bottom of the ocean."

"How can I be sure that you won't just let the bomb off afterwards?"

"Don't be an idiot!" the blackmailer said, starting to lose his patience with the man. "If that had been my intention, I would have done it by now. I don't like to see innocent blood spilled, so you have my word that as soon as Gus Callow has been thrown overboard I'll disconnect the bomb and you can throw it out to sea. Once ashore you just tell your boss that he fell over board and there was nothing you could do to save him."

"This is the devil's work!

"Don't you believe it. This system has already been tried and tested. Some media mogul whose name escapes me right now: Master, Marcel, Maxwell, or something like that; he went out on his yacht and disappeared in the middle of the night and nobody could ascertain whether it was a crime, an accident or suicide..."

The distraught captain thought for a second before calling over what appeared to be the head of Gus Callow's bodyguards. He opened up the cupboard and showed him the bomb, explained to him briefly what the situation was and told him that time was running out.

The hefty man barely blinked before heading straight for the stern, where he grabbed the unsuspecting fisherman by the neck and threw him head first in to the sea.

The captain simultaneously revved up the speed so that by the time the unhappy Dall&Houston board member had come up for air, waving his hands around and shouting for help, they were already fifty meters away.

Curiously, the enormous hook from one of the fishing lines that had been dangling in the water, caught on to one of his thighs so that he was dragged along behind them, howling with pain, leaving a trail of blood, until the bodyguard unhooked the line from its support and threw it in to the sea.

As the "Barracuda III°" moved out of sight, Gus Callow started to sink, pulled down by the weight of the heavy spool on the fishing line.

It was not long before the sharks smelled his blood.

Colorado, 2007

I called to my god and he did not reply.
I called him again and he remained silent.
After calling to him repeatedly I came to the bitter conclusion: my
parents' god was not the true god.
The Christian god seems so much more powerful.
But now I am here in a Christian country; in the most powerful
country of all, and I see the people praying to their god, and he does
not answer them either.
Where should I look now?
I am starting to fear that any such search might prove futile.

"When did you write this?"

"Last night."

"You never told me that you wrote."

"I've never done it before."

"Does it bother you that God may not exist?"

Salka Embarek took a while to answer. She examined the serene face of the old woman and said with absolute calm, "What worries me more is that he exists but allows all these things to happen. Do you believe in God?"

"Why should I?" she said adding, "Because I've reached an age where I should be clinging on by the skin of my teeth for any hope or sign that another life awaits me, or just because having seen so many things I might have lost all hope and need guidance."

"Have you lost hope?"

"To be honest, I've never really been under any illusion in that sense," Mary Lacombe admitted. "It's more that I've never really considered the possibility that there might be a superior being or a destiny that sets out our path. Everyone creates his or her own path and follows it. That's it really."

"Did you forge your own path?"

"Of course!" she snorted.

"And have you always stuck to it?"

"As much as I've been able to."

Salka was quiet for a moment. "And what is that path? We've spent days talking about me, but you've not told me anything about your life."

"Whatever I tell you about my past will hardly alter my future now," was her calm and slightly mocking reply. "When, however, you tell me something of yourself, what you were and what you might be tomorrow, it will have some impact."

"What?"

"At the moment you are here, fishing on the shores of a beautiful river and meditating calmly on the possibility of being adopted by some crazy old woman instead of wandering aimlessly from motel to motel, the vulnerable target of some old degenerate that wants to abuse you, or the police who want to catch you."

"You are right, it's just hard to accept, that's all."

"There are many other things that you'll start to accept with time. When you get to the last leg of the journey it's very painful to discover, as it is in my case, that you haven't anyone close to you that can carry on with the things you started building years ago. The instinct to reproduce isn't only about the need to continue a physical species, but from an intellectual point of view, the need to pass on all the knowledge that you have gathered throughout your life."

"I think I understand you, but I'm not sure."

"Put simply, my neurons are worth more to me than my genes are."

"Please be a little clearer, you have to remember that my school was blown up when I was only fourteen years old so I know very little about genes and neurons."

"I think it's perfectly clear!" the old lady muttered irritably.

71

"What I am trying to say is that I would prefer to have an intelligent person with me, that's not necessarily my own flesh and blood, than a fool, even if she were my own daughter."

"Do you think I am intelligent enough to be at your side?"

"That's what I'm trying to find out. But to be honest you still have some convincing to do," she replied curtly.

The girl did not say anything, went inside the caravan and came out with two drinks. After putting one in front of her companion she sat down at said:

"Well if you're looking for proof of intelligence then let's start right here: I have reached the conclusion that you are not called Mary Lacombe and you are not who you say you are at all."

"A curious theory. How did you get there?"

"Firstly because I haven't seen a piece of clothing or a ring, not even a bag or wallet with your initials on them, which is totally inappropriate for a woman. Secondly, because you have no idea how to even fry an egg or clean the bathroom or kitchen properly, which is strange since you have supposedly been a housewife. Thirdly, it is patently obvious that you are not used to serving anybody, not even breakfast, which doesn't add up if, as you say, you've been married, and lastly because you sleep sprawled across the bed, which proves that you have nearly always slept alone."

"None of those suspicions are conclusive darling."

"They wouldn't be in court, but we aren't in court. It's not about proof, but about a stacking up of small details that prove to me that you are hiding something. I don't have the faintest idea what that could be, however."

The old lady smiled weakly, as she said quietly, "It's true that we become careless in our old age."

"It's not age. It's just that with me you know you have nothing to fear."

"Haven't you just told me that you are a dangerous terrorist on the run from justice?"

"I'm beginning to think that I'm just a sad, unhappy person who's met up with just another sad and unhappy person."

Miami

Mauro Rivero's small, quaint shop where beauty concoctions were made and sold to the public at modest prices, (that mainly existed as a front for the rest of his businesses) was found one morning totally smashed up and covered in pro-Castro graffiti. Mauro Rivero said nothing but just sat down and looked on, as if totally devastated by the disaster, while his neighbours offered their condolences and the locals tried to rescue what little remained of the business.

He just repeated over and over again: "Why? What have I ever done to Castro's followers?"

His questions hung in the air unanswered. Mauro Rivero might have been many things, but a counter-revolutionary he was not.

Three days later, while balanced at the top of a ladder, dressed in an old boiler suit and immersed in the task of carefully painting the walls a light yellow, the ex-General Gilbert Espinosa appeared and looking around, asking repeatedly, "What the hell have you done to that mother fucker Fidel to make him want to do this to you?"

"Leaving La Havana too early maybe, before he was able to do anything worse." Mauro came down off the steps, left his brush on the counter and cleaning his hands with a cloth added, "Or maybe he just didn't like the idea of an exile getting on in another country without bothering anyone else."

"Why are you putting so much effort into this my friend? If you pick up the business again he'll just come back for more."

Mauro shrugged. "What else am I supposed to do, brother, give in?

"Stand up to him."

"That's what I'm trying to do by getting my business up and running again."

"That's not enough," Espinosa asserted. "We are here, working our asses off for our island and everything we love about it, struggling to provide a future for our children, while he, who has already displaced us by force and occupied our houses, waits until things have started to look up for us again and then sends in a new group of killers to destroy what we have rebuilt," the ex personal aid to Fulgencio Batista shook his head emphatically, totally lost in his own rhetoric. "No! We can't just offer up the other cheek. We have to go there and string him up by the balls."

Mauro Rivero picked up the paint brush again and waved it around like a banner, asking, "With what, with this? Don't make me laugh Espinosa. This "shit eater" is very well organised and armed to the hilt. Meanwhile, our famous exiles are just a bunch of big mouths that spend their time discussing war strategies whilst playing dominoes in the squares and bars of Little Havana."

"There are also some very well organised people out there that are taking the whole thing very seriously, which means we'll soon have powerful allies and arms, many arms!"

"I've never been a man of arms," said Mauro, "but as soon as you have them, tell me in case I decide to come and help you string this "shit eater" up by the balls."

"We need you now not then," was the ex-General's quick reply.

"Need me?" the businessman sounded surprised. "What do you need me for?"

"We know that you are not a man of arms, but we do know you are an extraordinary organiser, and astute manager, with the biggest and most well-informed ears in the whole of La Havana."

"What do you mean by that?"

"Oh come on Mauro, don't play the fool! It's well known that you created 'the Corporation' with a fistful of pesos and half a dozen friends and in the space of four years turned it in to the most influential organisation in Cuba. You were lucky that you knew what was going on and smart enough to get out of there in time. We are all convinced that you're starting off a new 'Corporation' here, which is already bringing you in quite a bit of money, despite the fact that you feel the need to repaint the walls of your 'honourable cosmetics business' yourself," he said wagging a finger at him and winking knowingly.

"Let's be practical," he added. "We need your 'Corporation', your informers and your organisational skills and you need us to get Fidel off your back. Let's work together."

Mauro Rivero, seemingly unperturbed, set about looking for a stick, which he found and started to mix the paint with until the lumps had disappeared completely, and then he resumed the task of painting the walls yellow again.

After just a few strokes and without turning round he said:

"Let me think about it for a few days!"

Los Angeles, 2007

It took Tony Walker about a week to contact Mariel's people in Los Angeles and another three days for them to agree to meet him. This meant that he would have to go through the usual rigmarole of being picked up by a car on the corner of his house, blindfolded, taken round the city and its backstreets for an hour, before parking in a garage that could have belonged to any house, anywhere in the city. He was then asked to remove his shoes, frisked over several times to make sure he had no radio signal on him and taken to a guarded room, where he waited for about forty minutes, until a hooded man, dressed entirely in black came and sat opposite him at the table.

"Good afternoon, Walker," the hooded man said in an extra-ordinarily deep and serious voice. "I'm sorry about all the fuss."

"I'm used to it, even if it is still a little annoying."

"You must understand that security is key to my work."

"That's why you are where you are," he agreed.

"Why have you come here?"

"A new contract."

"I told you that I'd decided to retire."

"I know, but my current boss thought that one hundred million might change your mind."

"That's a tidy sum, no doubt about it, but to be perfectly honest money is the only thing I've got too much off these days," the hooded man said, matter-of-factly. "Even if I live to seventy I won't manage to spend it all."

"I told my boss that, but I also said that with a bit of luck you might just be seduced by the challenge."

"I'm not interested in many challenges these days; at least very few. What's it about?"

"To try and find and destroy this terrorist that calls himself Aarohum Al Rashid."

"The one who's killing the guys on the board of directors for Dall&Houston?"

The other man nodded silently, as he continued:

"That's not so easy."

"That's what I mean when I say challenge's, and that why there's such a hefty reward."

"What makes them think I can do it where the FBI, the CIA and Blackwater have failed?"

"Exactly that. That you aren't the FBI, the CIA and much less Blackwater.

"The right answer, my man. Absolutely correct. But still, it's a difficult and dangerous job. From what I've heard, this man is very clever and tends to clean up after himself without leaving any leads."

"At the rate he's going, he'll have finished off the whole board of directors on schedule. Do you have any idea what it must be like for these poor guys to have this death sentence hanging over them that's as good as signed and sealed?"

"The word 'poor' doesn't really apply here," he said drily, "but yes I can imagine it must be difficult to come to terms with. Why don't they do what he's asking and rebuild Iraq, then just enjoy the rest of their money in peace for what's left of their time on this earth?"

"Will you do it?"

"At my age? I don't know, although I promise to give it some thought tonight," he said with a slight trace of humour in his voice. "I'd imagine that when Gus Callow found himself treading water in the middle of the ocean he would have been willing to hand over three hundred million dollars for a life jacket that would have only cost him ten dollars in a supermarket. Which goes to illustrate at what point the value of money stops being relevant. A few years ago I wouldn't have thought twice about killing twenty men for one hundred million, but it just doesn't motivate me anymore."

The hooded man paused for a long while, drumming his fingers on the table until finally, he reluctantly asked, "Do you know anything about this terrorist that could be useful to my investigations?"

"Nothing."

"Nothing?" he said, taken aback.

"Absolutely nothing," Tony Walker said, lifting up his hands in a despairing gesture. "Except for the fact that you're not dealing with a traditional terrorist here, because he kills with imagination and dangerous ease, which can't generally be said of that lot who tend to be a bit slapdash."

"How are the police dealing with the case?" the hooded figure changed tack.

"In a very disconcerting way. It's the first time they've come up against an assassin whose victims have only one thing in common: that they are all shareholders in a certain company."

"Their infamous special agents don't seem to have the faintest idea where to start."

"Certainly a criminal that is not motivated by sexual, political, or religious reasons, by revenge or greed, is atypical and therefore can't be pigeonholed as such. Do they really believe that all he wants to do is to rebuild Iraq?"

"That's what he's asking them to do."

"I'm not asking you about him but what the upper echelons at Dall&Houston think."

"Even amongst the upper echelons at Dall&Houston, opinions vary," Tony Walker admitted with a light shrug of his shoulders. "The situation's as clear as day. They are not going to return the money, so the only thing they can do now is to find the culprit or spend the next three months attending a rosary of funerals."

"Eleven by my calculation." He paused. "Are they really prepared to give me one hundred million without any guarantee of success?"

"Evidently. Look at what's at stake here, nothing less than their lives, and besides – the money is company money." Tony Walker shook his head in an agitated manner before concluding, "I'd imagine that they'll pay your expenses and wave any taxes."

The hooded man nodded. He took some time to cogitate then said, "All right! I'll call my people out of retirement and give it a go. I can't guarantee anything and I'd like the money up front."

"As always."

"As always."

Colorado, 2007

With the rain, the air cleared and the trout – apparently not fond of the change in climate – stopped taking their bait, and so the two women decided that the time had finally come for them to leave their camp and start the long journey to California, where, Mary Lacombe claimed, she had a home that was "more or less stable".

"The first thing I'm going to do when we get there is look for someone to teach you how to drive," she said. "In this country, not knowing how to drive is like not knowing how to walk."

"I'm not sure I'll be able to get my license," the girl said. "I'm hopeless with anything mechanical."

"You buy your license, my dear; you don't have to worry about that. The most important thing is that you learn how to drive well enough to make sure you don't wrap yourself round the first lamppost as soon as you're behind the wheel."

The first day on the road went smoothly enough, but on the second morning Salka Embarek was washing herself underneath a small waterfall, half hidden behind a cluster of rocks, when she realised she was being leered at by two men in uniform, who stood there, unashamedly drooling over the naked vision of beauty that stood before them. A month of good food and rest had transformed the girl from a skinny bag of bones into a woman with fuller breasts and buttocks, and a shiny mane of hair that fell half way down her back. Aware of their leery gaze, she forced herself to remain calm, put the soap down and stepped away from the water, intending to cover herself up, but the slimiest of the two men had already picked up her clothes.

"Maybe you didn't know that exhibitionism was illegal?" he leered.

"I have no interest in making an exhibition of myself, sir," she mumbled. "I was only washing." She faltered, "I checked to see that there was no one around…"

"Are you trying to say that we're no one?" he sneered.

"You must have been hidden since I didn't see you," she said firmly. "Please give me back my clothes."

"You'll have to come and get them."

Salka Embarek stretched out her hand, but the big man grabbed her wrist, forced her arm behind her back, and pushed her down on to her knees.

"Round here these kinds of favours are paid with another type of favour, young girl. Junior!"

The so-called junior went over straight away, handcuffed the girl's hands behind her back and held her down by her long hair while the other man stood behind her and started to take down his trousers as if she were a dog, saying, "If you stay calm it'll all be over with soon enough and you might even enjoy it, darling. Have you understood me gorgeous? Keep calm."

As if in response, a loud gunshot rang through the air followed by a cry of pain as the aggressor fell backwards, his face blown apart. He was dead before he hit the ground.

The agent that had answered to the name of junior turned round with his hand on his belt, looking for his gun, but stopped once he realised that a composed Mary Lacombe was right there, holding a high calibre gun to his chest and saying with surprising calm, "Don't even think about it."

Then pointing to the girl who was still on her knees, she shouted, "Let her go!"

He obeyed and opened the handcuffs with trembling hands. Once the victim was free the old lady said to the girl, "Take the gun off him!"

She waited for her to do so and then gestured for her to come and stand at her side, and after laying a hand on her shoulder as if trying to reassure her, she said, "Do you know how to shoot?"

The girl nodded. Then, in a voice that was devoid of all emotion, she said, "Kill him then."

"Kill him?" the disconcerted Salka Embarek ventured, "Just like that?"

"Just like that."

"Why?"

"Firstly, because in this state the penalty for killing a policeman, even if he's a son of a bitch that was about to rape you, is the death sentence and if we leave this one alive then there'll soon be another ten thousand of the same kind out there looking for an old woman and a girl, and they'll leave no stones unturned.

"Secondly, because I can't stand anyone who is supposedly in the job of overseeing that the law is upheld, who acts in blatant disregard of it, and I bet you this is not the first time these guys have done this.

"Thirdly, but no less importantly, I don't know you well enough to carry on with this journey, now you've witnessed me killing a policeman, unless of course I witness you doing the same thing."

"You can trust me. I would never to betray you to anyone."

"*Trust* is not a word that exists in my dictionary, little one, and in view of what's happened to you recently, I'd recommend you erased it from yours too," she paused, shrugging her shoulders as if the whole scenario was something of an aggravation.

"If you refuse to shoot then I'll have to do the same to you and rig up the scene to look like two honourable policemen came across a dangerous terrorist and they ended up killing each other."

"Are you really capable of doing that?" Salka Embarek asked, searching her companion's face for an answer, although in truth she knew the reply already.

"Yes, of course you're capable of doing so," she said, pulling down hard on the trigger. A black hole appeared in the middle of the man's terrified face.

"Good work!" the old lady said as their last victim fell to a heap.

Throughout the entire and bloody scenario she had remained entirely unmoved, as if killing two policemen was as simple and delicate a task as fishing for trout.

"From this moment on we're not only companions, but accomplices. What do you think?"

"Some people would think you're actually happy about all this," said Salka.

"Deep down I am happy. Sharing small secrets is the best way to consolidate a lasting friendship," said the old woman.

"Killing two police men doesn't strike me as a small secret at all," argued Salka Embarek. "I think it's more a case of you covering your back, because if we get caught it's the young and dangerous terrorist and not the poor defenceless old lady that's going down for pulling that trigger."

Miami

Mauro Riviera waited in the usual spot for Sandra "Bigmouth" to pick him up.

"We've got a bite," was the first thing he said. "And it's a big fat fish: General Gilberto Espinosa."

"The Butcher from Camaguey?"

"That very one."

"No way! We had our eyes on him and he was going to be one of our next targets," the ex-prostitute said, impressed.

"Well, he's best left alone for the time being as he's my only contact and I imagine that we're more concerned with getting details of the invasion than sending him to one of the Batista "butchers"."

"Too right!"

"Saved by the bell then. I think he believes in my good intentions, but it might be worth me giving him a convincing example of my future worth."

"Like what?" she enquired.

"Like giving him some kind of information that serves to convince him that I'm as efficient and trustworthy as he'd hoped."

"I can't think what."

"Think!"

"That's not one of my strengths."

"And what are your strengths?"

"Listening and being able to remember down to the last detail what is being said around me and doing exactly what I have been asked to do, having been told only once. I'm lucky, I have the memory of an elephant."

"In that case you must remember Asdrúbal Camacho, a regular client of the Papaya Verde."

She nodded as the Cuban added, "I suspect he works for

you."

"It's possible..." she replied without giving anything away.

"Well I've heard that he's working for the other side now."

"That might also be so..." Sandra "Bigmouth" replied in a neutral tone.

"In that case, you need to give me proof of any valuable information he might have passed on to you recently," said Mauro. "I can then pass it on to Espinosa and I'd imagine that should do the trick and I'll have won his trust completely."

"And what'll happen to the poor Camacho?"

"Those who play with a double barrel risk losing twice over."

"You're about to play with two barrels yourself."

"But I intend to keep all the aces to myself."

"In La Havana you were famous for being an extraordinary poker player, but I was told that General Contreras once won a small fortune against you."

"To lose at poker with Caraculo Contreras was the best investment anyone could possibly make in Cuba in those days," he said evenly. "It was just a more entertaining and discreet way of paying the commission he would otherwise have charged upfront for every new brothel opened and to ensure that he turned a blind eye to all of the shady dealings that went on in the casinos. He's not a bad player but very predictable because whenever he had a triple he'd go bright red and his cheeks were like watermelons."

"Ok, agreed," the Cuban girl nodded impatiently. "Let's move on. Sooner or later someone was going to bump Camacho off, and whether that's us or them is irrelevant. What matters is that his death will ensure you're welcomed in to the Rosas Blanca group with open arms."

"You can see that it all makes sense then."

"I'm not stupid," she snorted. "It's one thing not be able to think and another not to understand. There are people that think a lot and can understand pretty much anything related to their own thoughts, but have no idea how to process what other people are thinking at all.

"Well! Now you've left me out in the cold girl, but we're not here to waste time with riddles. Tell me something about Camacho that might be of some use to me."

"He told us that the "gusanos" have bought a cargo ship with a Panama registration called the Two Seas which will be used in the attack. We've located it in Puerto Rico but we're pretty sure that the invasion won't leave from there."

"Why?"

"Because Puerto Rico is a Free Associated State of the United States, and the gringos would never launch an attack against Cuba from their own territory. They'll probably choose Honduras, Nicaragua, Guatemala or Santo Domingo. That's what you need to find out, although I must stress that the day and the exact point of disembarkation is even more important."

"I'll do what I can," he agreed. "The information on this boat helps a lot."

Colorado

The old lady took the weapon from Salka Embarek, cleaned it very carefully and then threw it into the water, shouting orders all the while: "Get dressed and then try and get rid of the bare foot prints that you've left in the mud and your hand prints that you left when you were kneeling down. Take care to erase any evidence that shows there were two women here, because when this kind of thing happens they don't normally think of us women. I'll wait for you in the caravan."

But when the young girl arrived at the vehicle she saw that Mary Lacombe was not inside but standing fifty meters away speaking on the telephone, apparently in no hurry to leave, despite the fact that the two bodies of the policeman lay rotting in the sun nearby.

As soon as she had hung up, however, she started to move with some urgency and they gathered together their things speedily, meticulously erasing any evidence that might reveal that two women had spent the night there.

They spent the first part of their journey in absolute silence; a silence that lasted for more than a hundred miles, until the Iraqi girl could no longer keep it all in and had to ask, "What are we going to do now?"

"Forget the incident and never mention it again because we didn't provoke it. All that happened was that a pair of pigs were brought to justice. I used to be more tolerant, but like I told you, there's nothing I hate more in this world than the abuse of authority, especially by those whose job it is to uphold the law more than the rest of us."

"Do you really think that those two had done something like that before?"

"Quite probably, but that's not the point. Once is enough, and if I hadn't arrived just then you'd being going crazy right now thinking you could be pregnant or that you'd contracted some vile disease." She took her eyes off of the road for an instant and said curtly, "I would like to end the conversation regarding this unpleasant matter now. Subject closed."

This was a totally different Mary Lacombe from the one that shouted with joy each time she caught a trout, or the one who applauded herself or laughed, mockingly, every time she was dealt a good hand of cards.

This woman had very little in common with the harmless old lady who thought that everyone who lived in England must be personally acquainted with the Queen.

For the time being she drove in silence, as she sped down motorways, taking direction from a small GPS screen into which she had tapped some information as they had left, and that seemed to be directing them to a specific location that only she knew about.

After a couple of hours they left the motorway and took a series of back roads and tracks until they came out in to a small hollow where an enormous black Mercedes was parked.

Mary Lacombe stopped the caravan, waited until she had carefully checked that there was nobody about and only once she was convinced that they were totally alone did she park the vehicle and get out, whilst signalling to the girl.

"Get your things. Let's go."

She crouched down and looked under the back wheel of the Mercedes where she found the keys, which she used to open the trunk of the car.

"Whose is it?" Salka Embarek said, looking at the luxurious car.

"A friend's. Don't ask questions. Help me with this, it's heavy."

She was carrying two small plastic containers full of petrol that she had found in the car. She opened them both up straight away and began dousing the windows and inside of the caravan with petrol.

Within a few minutes, the vehicle that had been her home for the good part of a month, was burning like a flaming torch, as they walked away from it towards the Mercedes. The girl could only look back and watch as the caravan exploded, throwing out pieces of metal and wheels that burnt like fireworks.

Only once they had turned the corner and it was no longer in view did she venture to speak to her driver.

"You never fail to surprise me."

"Those people that fail to be surprised by others are usually very boring and end up being quite tiresome, little one," replied Mary Lacombe without taking her eyes off the road. "I should warn you that if you stick with me then there'll be more than a few surprises along the way."

"I don't want any more surprises for the minute. I've seen enough for the time being. I just need time to absorb all that's happened in the last twenty-four hours."

"Not much if it's anything compared with what you've told me about your life in Baghdad and the journey you made to get here. I didn't imagine fear would feature in your vocabulary after having gone through all that."

"Today wasn't about fear," she protested. "It was just discon-certing. What I lived through in Iraq was a war and the journey was crazy and kind of senseless, but I still don't know how to catalogue this one."

"What do you mean?"

"I mean that I've never seen anyone kill a human being and condemn another with such indifference and in such cold blood as you just did back there."

The old lady pulled over and stopped the vehicle in order to look at her companion more easily and then after a while she said gravely, "Listen to me carefully because it's time for you to decide on whether you stay with me or we go our own ways from here on out. It won't be worth mentioning what happened back there to anybody, which means that we can both head off in search of our individual destinies right now. Of course, we spent some unforgettable days together, but all good things come to an end, and you are, I promise you, free to go, with no hard feelings. If you decide to stay with me I'll give you everything I can, as long as you don't throw anything back in my face or judge me. I am what I am, I behave as I wish to behave, and I'll be the only one to pass judgement on my actions, if and when that is necessary, which in this case it is not. Am I making myself clear?"

"Very clear," she agreed, "although I'm not sure where this has all come from."

"It comes from the old tale of Cinderella and a fairy godmother who'll do anything you wish for, as long as certain conditions are met with along the way. Tell me what you want and I'll get it for you, but don't ask how I get it or why."

Miami

He was just finishing off a few details on the counter with a small paintbrush when the ex-General Gilberto Espinosa appeared, sat down on the same chair as before and, getting straight to the point, said: "It's been three days. What have you decided?"

Mauro Rivero sat down on an empty box, put his paintbrush to one side and started to clean his hands with a black cloth, all the while shaking his head in a gesture that indicated he was far from keen on the visitor's proposal.

"I'd rather not get involved in something so risky," he said. "I've made some enquiries and reached the conclusion that the famous 'White Rose' brigade is not foolproof enough."

"What do you mean?" Espinosa asked.

"That it's not going to work because your people talk too much, which means that we'll be blown up as soon as we land on the island. In fact I might even go as far to say that we'll be blown up before then."

"What the hell are you referring to?" the ex-General asked in an alarmed tone.

"That the Castro bunch know the name of one of the boats that you're planning to take your army to Cuba in and where it is docked. They're watching it day and night and they'll sink it, with weapons and know-how as soon as it leaves for open water."

"Who exactly found out all this?" he asked suspiciously.

"Me."

"You found it out?"

"Of course, Gilberto," Mauro Rivero replied calmly. "Of course! What do you think I live off? This shop and the sale of my creams that clear the skin and untangle the hair? Part of my organisation remains intact in Havana and I'm aware of everything that's going on in Miami. If it only took me three days to find out one of your biggest military secrets, then how long do you think it would have taken for the Castro bunch to find out?"

"I don't believe it!"

"Believe what you want, but I advise you to get rid of the Two Seas, a cargo ship with a Panama flag that's currently docked in San Juan, Puerto Rico."

"Shit…! It's not possible! How did you get that information?"

"I already told you that it's my job to find out things, and modesty aside, I consider myself to be the best in the field…" he said, shrugging his shoulders as if that was information enough, adding, "For that reason and because I don't want them to do to me what they did to my shop, I would rather not involved in something that has such a small chance of success."

"I can understand all that and your decision," the ex-general admitted, clearly taken aback by the news. "Do you have any idea who might have given this information to Castro's lot?"

"Yes."

"And that is…?"

"To hand over that information would mean making enemies and as you must understand, it would be stupid of me to go looking for those. I think I've done you a favour by warning you that you've got moles in the ranks who are working for Fidel and that's enough. You can't ask me to risk my neck for the love of art. It's not my style."

"What is your style then?"

Mauro Rivero took out a one hundred dollar bill from his pocket and waved it around in the air, smiling mischievously, saying, "This is my style, Gilberto, and you know it. Lots of these! If you really think you've got a chance of winning and returning to La Havana, which is where I would really rather be as well, since I'm never going to be more than a bastard exile here, I would work for free for you, but looking at how chaotic your organisation is, I'm not keen, so I either charge for it or stay on the sidelines."

"Has anyone ever told you you're a son of a bitch, with all due respect to your mother, who I am told is suffering from ill-health?" the ex-general enquired with a faint smile, as if trying to play down the cruel nature of his question.

"Yes, I'm quite accustomed to being called that, but it's not something that bothers me because I know my mother's a decent woman."

"How much for the name?"

"Ten thousand dollars."

"I'm sure you realise that I don't carry that amount of money around with me," the other man replied. "Will you accept a cheque?

"Will you accept a deal whereby if the cheque can't be cashed then I'll get one of my men to shoot you?"

"Of course!"

"In that case make it out..." he said.

The ex-general to Fulgencio Batista did as he was told, signed the cheque and gave it to Mauro Rivero, who put it straight into the pocket of his boiler suit without even looking at it and said nonchalantly, "Your mole is called Asdrúbal Camacho."

"Camacho? Goalkeeper for the Añoranza de Cuba team?" he said and making a silent gesture of disbelief exclaimed, "Son of a bitch! Are you sure?"

"Entirely. I wouldn't send a person to their death if there were any doubt over their innocence. I can tell you that he's working for you and Fidel."

"Right! Asdrúbal Camacho is a dead man. Would you reconsider working for us if we sorted him out?"

"I'd have to think about it.And above all I would have to make sure that there weren't any more Camachos in your ranks. In short, an objective like this, which aims to overthrow a government that has fought tooth and nail to get in to power, has to put security at the top of its list. Without that security guaranteed I'm not sure I want to risk my neck."

Texas

Belem de Para - Agency

On the last recorded sixth day, river police intercepted the passage of the cargo boat "Porto de Moz" in Amazon waters, on suspicion of transporting cocaine from Columbia.

When the cargo was checked, however, they were surprised to find that that it was not carrying cocaine, but forty tonnes of coltan, a mineral that is a key component in some industry processes, and not one which was known to exist in our country, other than in very small quantities.

The authorities interrogated the captain of the "Porto de Moz" as to the origin of such a large amount of the mineral, but all he could say was that he had simply followed orders from the boat's owner and that the boat had been loaded in the small port of Bonlugar where he imagined it had arrived there aboard other river barges.

Since there is no existing law in Brazil that prohibits the traffic of coltan, they allowed the cargo ship to continue its passage to New York.

The president of Dall&Houston very carefully placed the press clipping that he had just read out loud on to the table, tried to smooth out a crease in the paper, cleared his throat a few times and finally, without lifting his head, said, "I've called a meeting because this piece of news means that we may have to change our plans, or at least hurry them along. Unfortunately we didn't take into account the fact that cocaine isn't just produced in Colombia, but Peru, Bolivia and Ecuador, which means that their obvious route out to sea would be via the Amazon rivers and their multiple tributaries. This means that our mineral cargos are at risk of being discovered."

"Can't we just bribe the port authorities?" Jeff Hamilton said. "The Brazilians are famously corrupt."

"They'll just suspect us of drug trafficking and they're very strict in that respect," came the president's quick reply. "What we're trying to get them to do is check the boats but not tell anyone what's in them, or where they've come from."

"Where do they actually come from, if I might ask?" the normally quiet Judy Slander asked.

"For the time being you can't know," the president replied in a surprisingly serious tone.

"We're currently negotiating the transfer of huge areas of land for a maximum of forty years, but logically the Brazilian government will raise the stakes if it catches on that there are important deposits of coltan in the area."

"Will they accept the transfer of so much land to foreigners in Brazil?" Jeff Hamilton enquired. "I had the feeling they were quite reticent about these things."

"Up to now we've used companies with local money and we are convinced that the government will accept our offer if we guarantee that we won't cut down the forests, keep ninety per cent of the jungle in its actual state, and go about gradually reforesting it. For the Brazilians, as well as for many ecological organisations, one of the main reasons behind climate change has been the brutal and indiscriminate deforestation of this Amazon bowl, which has been the victim of unscrupulous and totally lawless poachers, so they should view anyone who invests and agrees by contract not to destroy more than is absolutely necessary, in a very good light."

"How much land are we talking about here?"

"About forty thousand hectares."

Judy Slander let out a short whistle of admiration. "That's outrageous! Are we thinking of founding a new country?"

"Of course not! But if we are trying to get control of

production then we have to stop other investors from immediately buying up any land close by. Coltan is incredibly capricious but we have to go with the idea that if it shows up in one determined area then there must be more of it around close by. I'd rather take preventative measures than regret it."

"They seem like logical precautions."

"That's why we're here today. We need to have one thing clear: in the near future, whoever controls coltan, controls the world. Raise you're hand if you're in on this investment."

"How much is it?"

"We're currently in discussion with the authorities, but I'm confident it won't exceed ten billion, that is to say a tenth of what we earned from Iraq."

Peter Corkenham paused briefly, before adding, "And I can guarantee that if all goes to plan, we'll get even better results this time."

"It could be interesting," Hamilton admitted.

"It's very interesting," the president said curtly. "I await your decision."

One after the other, the surviving members on the Dall&Houston board of directors put up their hands in support of the project, which the president acknowledged with a slight nod of his head, before pressing the interphone at his side. "Get Tony Walker to come in."

Walker appeared in the room almost immediately and his host gestured for him to sit down in one of the empty chairs, saying, "As many of you know, Tony had decided to retire, but I've convinced him to come back to work because I think that he's the only one that can help us sort out the problem of this crazy terrorist, who's intent on getting rid of us..." he nodded in the direction of his guest and said, "Over to you."

The man being asked to address them took a few minutes before speaking, aware that for everyone there, what he was about to say was of primordial importance as their lives depended on it.

"As you all know, there have been four casualties in one month..." he finally began. "And at the moment no one has the remotest idea who Al Rashid is. However, what we do know is that he is a man of many means and a lot of external help, although so far we haven't been able to link anyone to him, not even as an accomplice."

"Well, I don't believe Gus Gallow died as the captain of the boat claimed he did..." Jeff Hamilton pointed out. "It smells fishy and we need to tighten the screws, on him and the bodyguards."

"Not you or anyone else," admitted Walker. "But 'extra officially' I've been given a version of events that I feel obliged to accept. It seems that there was a bomb on board the boat, and hey were forced to act under the knowledge that it was either Gus Callow's life or all of them, including Gus, who should never have risked going sailing under those circumstances, just as you had advised against it. Bearing this in mind, I think that this matter should now be closed."

"It's easy for you to say when it's not your neck on the line," Judy Slander muttered.

"For that reason alone – that my head is not on the line – I can be more impartial and able to analyze the situation with a cool head," came his sharp and slightly impatient response. "I have managed to see Mariel personally, who you've all heard about, and he has already started work on the case. But in the mean time it is quite absurd that you continue to lead your lives as normal, as if nothing was happening. The only way that we can protect you is if you stick together until this son of a bitch is caught."

"Are you suggesting that we should live together?" Vincent Kosinsky was one of the few of the board that had not said a word throughout the meeting. He was a man renowned for his love of gambling, alcohol and woman and precious little else. Even though he often seemed to be in another world, he never missed a trick and those that knew him could testify that, when he was not drunk, his brain was like an enormous computer that classified and registered every last detail.

"That's what I said. We're looking for a place where you will be comfortable but safe for the moment."

"A safe place?" he repeated, clearly annoyed. "Are you referring to a type of fortress; Alcatraz, or an island lost in the Pacific?"

"Call it what you want."

"Personally, the safest place for me is my suite at the Cactus Flower, and I'm not prepared to change my habits and turn myself in to a caveman for anybody. I'd rather die before I'm buried."

"Well, it has been demonstrated that not three, or four, not even a dozen of the best Blackwaters have been able to stop the killings. If you carry on acting as you are now, you cannot guarantee your safety. Not here, nor in the most well guarded casinos in Las Vegas."

"Are you insinuating that we have to lock ourselves up while this terrorist runs free?" intervened Jeff Hamilton, clearly disconcerted. "That's ridiculous!"

"Locked up alive or dead and buried, that's for you to decide. All I can do is advise you and find a safe place for you to be."

"But what about our families, our children, spouses, and our friends ...?" Judy Slanders asked incredulously. "Our businesses ...? It's crazy?

"I suppose that Marzan, Sandorf, Medrano and Gus Callow would rather be sacrificing a bit of fresh air right now, than rotting underground," was the reply. "In the meantime, that is all I have to say, and those of you that decide you want to be somewhere safe, let me know as soon as possible so that I can get on with finding you a hiding place that is totally impenetrable."

Miami Beach

Asdrúbal Camacho was killed in what the police described as an attempted armed robbery. A week later the White Rose's main players met with Mauro Rivero in one of the private salons at the Shelborne Hotel on Miami Beach. Although they were at first reluctant to accept the total clean out of their ranks that he was proposing, his powers of persuasion soon started to sway the mood of most of the people present at that small meeting.

"Of those that make up the list that I've put together..." he started to say, with customary calm, "At least about twenty have close relations in Cuba, which means that Fidel's agents can pressurize them to give over information by threatening to take reprisals," he said, underlining three names with his pen before continuing, "These here are real crooks who you shouldn't even buy a used car from; not even a second hand bicycle. The rest I consider to be capable of lighting a fuse or shooting, but not suitable for preparing a landing, which requires very precise logistics and extraordinary stealth, otherwise there won't be a puppet left with his head on the moment we set foot on that island."

"But you've got about fifty names there..." the ex-General Contreras protested. "I think you're a bit ahead of yourself here, Mauro."

"In this case it's better to be over the top now than be cut short at the end," came his sharp response. "We're not playing poker in Havana right now and I'm not going to let you win, knowing that you have only a pair when I've got a triple hand of kings. We are playing with the lives of hundreds of boys that will come face to face with an army that has already pushed them back out to sea once before. I'm warning you, the reason they did that with such great ease was because you'd been infiltrated, even in your higher ranks. Or have you forgotten about Ruperto Barcenas, who was your third in command, and who later became one of the most conspicuous bigwigs in the Revolution?"

"Don't remind me of Barcenas. Rotten son of a bitch!"

"Those who choose not to learn from their mistakes, run the risk of making the same one again, my brother," the Cuban warned. "I don't want anything to do with someone that trips over the same stone twice. You cut this lot out or I'm going home."

"But fifty…"

"Since there are one hundred," intervened Gilberto Espinosa, "Mauro is right, and in any case this was starting to look like a negro's tea party. If we want Kennedy to back us, or the CIA to give us some money and arms, then we have to give the impression that we're a serious and well-organised outfit."

"The CIA organisation isn't all it's trumped up to be either," said an anonymous voice.

"Even more reason then. For our partners to trust us, we have to be doubly sure of our own people. I agree with Mauro that we must limit the amount of people that know anything, to as few as possible."

The discussion continued for some while and at times it became heated, but then a strange thing began to happen. Little by little a united front started to emerge among those who had suffered first hand, the embarrassment of having been expelled from their own land and then that of being hopelessly defeated in the attempted invasion that had been backed by the Dominican dictator.

The unflappable Mauro Rivero gave a few more examples of his incredible ability to pretend and seduce, all the while maintaining an air of absolute indifference, or rather sticking adamantly to the fact that he was not at all interested in taking part unless every angle had been covered to ensure that the organisation could arrive on safe shores.

In truth, the reason behind his success was not so much to do with his ability to pretend, but because his total indifference was genuine and it did not matter to him whether he was deceiving the Castro opposition or their enemies, as he was only ever really concerned with the end result. He was still the lizard-child that basked in the sun, who never broke a sweat and observed the world from a distance. Human passion was so alien a concept to him that he may as well have been born a cold-blooded animal.

There are people who pride themselves on being able to see right through a person at first glance, but even the most skilled of those would be probably admit defeat were they ever faced with this incredibly indifferent person.

He was like the "Gunslinger", acted by Yul Brynner in that unforgettable film Westworld, where he played a robot programmed to start duels. Mauro Rivero, however, did not have a soul made of metal, he simply did not have one at all.

If someone stuck a knife in him, he would bleed; if someone shot him, he would probably die; but neither of those events would alter his demeanour an inch.

After a Pantagruelian lunch, by the outdoor pool on the beach, during which time they had sampled about twenty different Californian wines, the meeting was resumed and onlookers would have been forgiven into believing that the White Rose members, however anxious to recoup power in Cuba, had not the faintest idea about how to go about it. But finally they had found someone who was full of ideas and clarity. Who was sharp enough to reveal details about their own people that they had failed to notice, which included the now defunct Asdrúbal Camacho, who had been dealt with in forty-eight hours. They now had reason to believe, for the first time ever, that they had some hope of winning.

The meeting ended with unanimous shouts of: "Long live Cuba! Long live a free Cuba! Long live Cuba, free of Fidel!"

Los Angeles

When she awoke she had no idea where she was.

She knew that she must have been asleep for a very long time as the last thing she remembered was eating in a small restaurant, that overlooked the infinite lights of Los Angeles below, and then getting into the car and just closing her eyes, her body consumed by an unbearable heaviness, as if she had been drugged.

The sun was already high in the sky and coming in at angles through the slats of the blind. The bedroom was enormous; she had never seen one so big, and certainly not more luxurious, with a bed that four people could comfortably sleep in and furniture the likes of which she had only seen in American films.

She remained quite still, a thousand questions racing around her mind, which was still a little confused due to the effects of the drug that had made her sleep. She was unsure of whether to get up and explore this wonderfully lavish place, or stay put and enjoy being in the most comfortable bed she had ever been in. After a while Mary Lacombe opened the door and walked in. She went straight over to the balcony and opened the doors slowly, allowing the rays of sunlight to flood in, revealing an ocean that stretched right out to the horizon before her.

"Good morning sleepyhead," she said cheerfully. "It's time to return to the land of the living."

"Did you give me something that made me sleep?"

"Naturally."

"Why?"

"I thought that for the moment it was best that you didn't know the way to my house."

"By night and in Los Angeles?"

"You never know. Sometimes, but not always, you can be very clever."

"Is this your house?" she asked. When Mary Lacombe replied with a silent nod, she continued, "And is this your bedroom?"

"Oh no, my dear! This is one of the guest rooms, although I've never had any guests to stay before."

"Why do you have guest rooms if you never have anyone to stay in them?" she asked.

"The bedrooms were here when I bought this tiny place," Mary Lacombe, said smiling broadly as she sat down on the edge of the bed. "What would you like me to do with them?"

The girl did not answer but got up and went to the bathroom, which was bigger than her living room in Baghdad. She flushed the lavatory, washed her face and cleaned her teeth, using all the things she found on the shelves. Walking back in to the bedroom she went over to the balcony to take in the view and realized that they were on the edge of a high cliff.

"You must be incredibly rich," she eventually whispered.

"I am."

"In that case, with a house like this, what on earth are you doing chugging around the world like a tramp in that caravan?"

"It's a long story and one I don't yet feel ready to tell you, apart from the fact that I thought that caravan was truly wonderful. Would you believe me if I said that I preferred bumbling around the country in that, than I do being imprisoned up here for months in this mausoleum?"

"Why wouldn't I believe you?"

"I'm not sure; maybe because most people prefer the security of four walls and the luxury of Persian rugs. Tomorrow I'll go and buy another caravan."

"I doubt they make those any more."

"In that case I'll get one made up especially."

The Iraqi girl did not reply but went over to an armchair and sat down, observing her companion for some time before finally enquiring:

"Where does all this come from? When will you tell me the

truth about yourself?"

"When I think you're ready to know the truth. For the moment be happy in the knowledge that you can ask for whatever you want."

"How about breakfast?"

The old lady pressed a button above the bedside table and a few seconds later a maid in uniform opened the door, and came in pushing a small trolley full of delicious looking food.

"Good morning," she said politely.

"Good morning."

"Would you like coffee or tea?"

"Tea please."

"Milk? Sugar?" the maid responded to a silent nod of the head and served breakfast on the balcony, putting a chair next to the table for her to sit on.

"Fried or scrambled eggs?"

"Scrambled."

An hour later, after having explored the stately house that was surrounded by carefully tended gardens and protected by high walls and electric fences, Salka Embarek sat down in one of the hammocks by the swimming pool and asked:

"How did you end up with all this?"

"By working hard and saving a lot," the owner of the house answered evasively.

"You lie too much," her companion retorted. "So much so that I don't think you've told me one single piece of truth in the last couple of days... and I don't like it. I have already been manipulated to the point where I was ready to blow myself up, and I don't want to repeat that again. I'm not that stupid."

"Listen to me carefully, little one..." Mary Lacombe said pointedly. "In your bedside table there is a revolver because in this cursed city, where rapists, robbers and murderers run amok, it's always a good idea to have one within arm's reach. If one day you reach the conclusion that I am manipulating you to my advantage and not to your own, then I give you permission to shoot me and then you can disappear off, as the same suspected fugitive terrorist that you were before we met, only this time round you'll have the added bonus of having the murder of a policeman on your list, so I doubt that one more murder would make much difference to your overall predicament."

"Make fun of me if you want, but they say that the first time you are deceived you can blame the deceiver. The second time it happens, however, it's your own fault. I don't deny that the disconcerting events that have taken place over the last few days have left me feeling confused, but knowing me, I am confident that the time will come when I'll be able to make sense of all this and if I don't like what I see I'll just shoot you point blank."

"I wouldn't expect anything less of you. Had I thought you were anything less than courageous, you wouldn't be here now."

"You mean you're looking to adopt a courageous daughter?"

"Of course!"

"Why?"

"Because if you weren't intelligent or brave then you wouldn't be able to protect what has cost me so much to obtain and when the day comes for me to pack it all in, I want to do so in the knowledge that all my efforts haven't been wasted."

"But they won't have been wasted anyway as they helped you to get a place like this. I can't believe that there are many people in the world that have a house like this, just outside of Los Angeles. What else, I ask you, could really happen once you've gone?"

"Good point, darling. Really very good! 'No use flogging a dead horse' and all that. But I've always hated banks and the very thought that they might get all my money without having ever lifted a finger for it makes my blood boil. I'd rather fill up the swimming pool with it all and burn it, than let them have it, I swear."

Texas

"Listen to what Leonardo da Vinci had to say:

"Creatures will been seen on earth who will always be fighting against each other with great losses and frequent deaths on both sides and there will be no end to their malice. By their strong limbs we shall see a great portion of the trees of vast forests laid low throughout the universe; and, when they are filled with food, the satisfaction of their desires will be to deal death and grief and labour and wars and fury to every living thing; and from their immoderate pride they will desire to rise towards heaven, but the too great weight of their limbs will keep them down. Nothing will remain on earth, or under the earth or in the waters, which will not be persecuted, disturbed and spoiled, and those of one country removed into another. And their bodies will become the sepulchre and means of transit of all they have killed."

"In another of his many quotes he says of metals:

"They shall be brought forth out of dark and obscure caves, which will put the whole human race in great anxiety, peril and death...O monstrous creature! How much better would it be for men that they be returned to Hell! For this the vast forests will be devastated of their trees; for this endless creatures will lose their lives"."

"How could Leonardo, genius that he was, have made such accurate predictions five hundred years ahead of his time?"

"Maybe he knew we'd end up discovering coltan and that its appearance on the face of the earth would mean the beginning of the end."

"Do you really think this is the beginning of the end?"

"It seems that way," Tony Walker said. "However many

promises you might have made to the Brazilian government, you'll still have to cut down an infinite numbers of trees if you're going to get out as much of this mineral as you claim you will."

"Each tree will be replanted immediately."

"And how long will it take for that tree to grow to the same height? Eighty years, one hundred, two hundred years, maybe? I recently read that the Amazon plain is made up of a clay mass which is full of nutrients, but torrential rains are carrying it out to the rivers, which are then carried out to sea, fast turning it in to one of the most barren regions on earth. It cannot replenish itself and when your people leave there, you will leave behind you a land that is good for nothing. Da Vinci was right."

"Why bother trying to protect it then? If it's not us, it'll be someone else that pulls up the trees, because there's no way that if there's coltan there it'll stay in the ground for long. First come first served. That's life."

"It reminds me of an old poem: '*It makes me weep to imagine a world without valleys, mountains or riverbanks, where flocks of sheep can go to quench their thirst...*'" Tony Walker said in a voice full of disillusion, adding, "What are we going to leave behind for our future generations?"

"Mobile telephones and guided weapons. But we didn't start all this, my dear friend, we've simply been caught up in it, and tried to keep ahead simply to avoid getting crushed along the way. Talking of being crushed: Any news of our good friend Mariel? Has he managed to find out anything else about Al Rashid?"

"That, despite his name, he's not a Muslim."

"What's this?"

"Because the first two murders, those of Marzan and Sandorf, were carried out during the month of Ramadan, and the second one was actually committed on a Friday, a day of rest and therefore sacred. In his opinion, no Muslim, above all one that is seeking justice, would choose those dates to commit murder on, when the rest of the year is available."

"Interesting theory! What do you think?"

"That it's better than nothing and if we rule out the Muslims, I suppose it only leaves us with around five or six billion suspects...."

"You don't seem very optimistic."

"My grandfather told me that optimism has taken more people to the grave than pessimism and history has taught us that there aren't many reasons to be optimistic, while there are plenty of reasons to be pessimistic. But better to be safe than sorry, so for the meantime I recommend that you stay locked up at the ranch, because as soon as you step foot outside of there, nobody, not the Blackwater bunch nor anyone else, can guarantee your safety."

"And what kind of a life do you think that is, shut up between those four walls the whole time?"

"Graves are narrower, Peter, I promise you... much narrower."

Las Vegas

Vincent Kosinsky had lived in the same luxurious suite for many years, on the top floor of the Cactus Flower, one of the oldest and most famous casinos in Las Vegas.

It did not cost him anything, or better said, he did not pay anything to live in this splendid place, since the amount he lost every year at dice, roulette, horse racing or betting of any kind, could have bought him ten houses, a thousand times bigger and more luxurious, so the establishment's management figured it was more lucrative to keep the eccentric millionaire in-house rather than risk losing him and his money to Cesar's Palace or The Miracle.

The always smiling, chatty and vivacious, Vicent Kosinsky had lived, since time immemorial, according to his one and only rule:

"Money is for playing around with and if there's any left, squander it".

He was, therefore, not only the casino's best client, but the best client at the city's many other bars, restaurants and brothels.

With no known dependents and lucky at everything except gambling, Kosinsky had always managed to sniff out a good investment, and had therefore successfully converted a large fortune inherited from his father into a lavish income, which he happily shared around and threw away during his infamously eccentric and wild shenanigans.

His habit of eating, drinking, fornicating and gambling for days on end, with out a break, had turned him in to a legendary character in an already legendary Las Vegas. So it came as no surprise to anyone that when Tony Walker suggested that they all went to live in a refuge, miles from anywhere in order to be safe from the dangers posed to them by the terrorist, he refused point blank, saying that he would rather be dead than buried alive.

Even so, he still made a point of meeting with his old friend Gigi Trotta and asked him:

"What would happen if your best client, the compulsive gambler that leads a famously dissolute life, was murdered in the casino that you run."

"My father would not hesitate to kick me out and put me in charge of the parking lot," he said.

"In that case, my respected and appreciated Gigi, if you're interested in keeping your position, as I imagine you are, I advise you to triple security, especially on the top floor."

"From tonight onwards I'll just have the men that are here to protect you, staying in the casino," Gigi Trotta said and pointing his finger defiantly, he added, "I give you my word that our men and waiters will be looking after you twenty-four hours a day, but you must assure me that you won't cause a scene every time one of my boys tries to get the prostitutes coming up to your room, to sign in."

"I want them searched, not signed in!"

"They are used to that Vincent! Very used to it! Some of them sleep with my security men, which is why I never understand them playing the virgin when the same security men try to put their hands between their legs. We only do it to make sure they're not armed."

"Don't worry, I won't complain."

"And another thing; try and see if you can break your awful habit of going out on to your balcony, drunk and naked in the middle of the night and peeing on the heads of passers by. Apart from the bad image it gives us, anyone could take a shot at you from Cesar's Palace."

"I'll turn off the lights."

"These days there are rifles with telescopic night vision, dear boy, and gunmen with infinite patience, capable of blowing your balls off from around seven hundred meters away, and by that I mean your balls!"

Vincent Kosinsky, as wild and dissolute as he was, was incredibly smart, so he met with the requests of his old friend and stopped creating a scene every time one of his whores was signed in and refrained from going out to pee from his balcony at night or during the day, and installed himself semi-permanently in the Cactus Flower's private salons, which only allowed in a very select few, where he threw himself into a revelry of non-stop gambling.

He attended to his numerous businesses, on occasion, by telephone or by computer.

The following week, however, and in spite of the infinite precautions that they had taken, Vincent Kosinsky was found dead in his bathroom. When Gigi Trotta enquired about the cause of death of his best client and friend, a smirking policeman said:

"From what our forensics have been able to deduce, he was killed by 'dendrobatids'."

"What the hell are they?" the managing director of the Cactus Flower enquired. "Another Islamic terrorist group?"

"I've just learnt that they are poisonous frogs that live in the humid and rainy South American jungle, from Nicaragua to Bolivia. It seems that there are some two hundred different species, and during their metamorphosis, which is when they change from a tadpole into an adult frog, they grow glands whose main function is to keep the skin moist, but that also secrete antibiotic substances, biogenics and toxins. Certain species produce a special type of poison that has toxic properties similar to those found in nicotine, morphine and cocaine."

"Are you talking double Dutch?" interrupted the perplexed listener. "Did I ask for a lesson in zoology at nine o'clock in the morning at such an inappropriate moment?"

"According to the doctors, and I've only overheard this, the frog called Epipedobates Tricolor, which comes from Ecuador, produces an analgesic, two hundred times stronger than morphine and capable of killing a man in one go. This Tricolor is what killed your guest."

"And how the hell did an "Epipo" bloody "Tricolor" get into the bathroom other than by my putting it there."

"In a bar of soap."

"In a bar of soap?" the hotel director repeated incredulously. "What do you mean "in a bar of soap"?"

"Just what I said. Somebody injected the poison from this mangy little reptile into the bar of soap, which, once dissolved, covered the body of that poor guy Kosinsky in poison."

"You're joking!"

"I'm not. It's all true. A small amount must have slipped into his body by his nose, ears or anus... what do I know! Maybe it was enough just to have absorbed it through the skin. In any case, he would have collapsed and died seconds later."

"Oh Christ! What's going to become of me?"

"Don't worry!" the officer said, trying to calm him down. "Officially we'll record the death as a heart attack, which isn't that far from the truth as I doubt anybody's heart could cope with an attack of that kind."

"Why the deference?"

"It's not deference. It's just not in our interests for it to get out that a millionaire under protection was murdered in one of our Las Vegas casinos," he clicked his tongue as if the whole incident had been quite a nuisance, before concluding, "It's even more important that it doesn't get out that all you have to do to get rid of someone these days is travel to South America, get hold of a few of these deadly frogs and send the victim a bar of soap, a bottle of cologne, deodorant or whatever with the poison inside it. We've got enough on our plate without these so-called 'dendrobatids' adding to it all."

"Who could have injected the poison in to the soap?"

"That, we have yet to find out."

Miami, 1961

"The CIA and the White Roses have jointly recruited about one thousand five hundred volunteers, most of whom are Cuban exiles and mercenaries, trained in Guatemala, Puerto Rico and Nicaragua. They make up what they call 'Brigade 2506', which consists of artillery men, paratroopers and pilots, and they have a fleet of boats and planes, donated to them by the Americans," he pointed to the book and said. "Take note: fourteen transport planes, sixteen bombers, five tanks, thirty canons, fifteen jeeps, some mortars, twelve lorries and seven landing craft..."

Mauro Rivero paused briefly while Diana "Bigmouth" finished taking notes and when he considered it opportune, he continued, "The plan reveals that the first armed boat will set off from Nicaragua, preceded by aerial attacks which will aim to annihilate your air force by destroying your planes on the ground as well as the runways. When the supply and support planes land, the paratroopers will disembark and take control of the roads in the area..."

"But where exactly will they land?" she interrupted.

"In the Bay of Pigs, specifically the Girón beach and three days later a Provisional Government will be put in place which will then make a formal request to the United States for military assistance. The area was chosen because it is not easily accessed by land and what they hope to do is delay the arrival of your army, since while they are defending this territory they expect there to be desertions."

"There will not be any desertions!"

"There *will* be," contradicted Mauro Rivero. "Three pilots that take part in the attack will carry on to Miami, their planes will have the Cuban flag painted on them and they will claim to be Castro deserters so that the United States will take them under their wing and claim there is an *'internal conflict'* on the island."

"Bloody sons of bitches! Whose idea was that?"

"Mine."

"You bastard!"

He gave him an envelope saying: "Here you have files on the three pilots that will have supposedly deserted you, with photos of them training in Puerto Rico and taking orders from gringo teachers, which will of course, ridicule any grandiose statements that the Americans decide to make."

"You're so weird and twisted! And full of surprises. When do you expect all this to kick off?"

"On the dawn of April fifteenth, but you have to warn your people not to bother with the first troops that land; they don't pose a risk. The first thing that the Castro army has to do is sink the Houston and Hidden River boats, which will be sailing about thirty thousand miles off the coast towards Mexico, which appear to be inoffensive but are actually carrying heavy armaments. Without this equipment the invaders won't survive on land for longer than three days."

"If all this is true, and I'm sure it is, otherwise – as you well know – you're a dead man, you've done a magnificent job."

"In that case you owe me some money."

Diana "Bigmouth" turned around in her seat and picked up the suitcase that was tucked underneath it, and gave it to him.

"You've earned it."

"He opened it, checked the amount and then without a hint of recrimination and with his usual measured calm added: "There's something missing."

"Not that I am aware of," she said equally calmly.

"You wouldn't know about it because I didn't mention it, but in order for everything to run perfectly we have to take care of one last detail."

"And that is...?"

"My death."

Her enormous mouth fell wide open.

115

"What did you say?" she finally stammered.

"What I mean is that if everything goes to plan and as long as between now and then we don't have any nasty surprises, it would be best for me if I was 'shot down by enemy bullets' during the landing."

"Really?"

"Are you totally stupid or what?" Mauro Rivero spat, without looking up. "How could that really happen? What's important is that I appear later in the lists of casualties and that a few weeks later a body is sent to my mother, so decomposed that she won't recognize me, apart from this ring that she gave me when I was fifteen."

He took off the ring that he was wearing on his little finger and put it in to the palm of "Green Papaya's" ex employee and carefully closed her fingers over it saying:

"Look after it! My future depends on it. If I don't die then the White Rose lot will assume that it was me who grassed."

"But what about your mother?"

"She won't be that bothered, and if she is then she'll be pleased to know that her son died trying to reclaim her beloved patria, rather than by a shot to the head for being a traitor."

"The mother that gave birth to you."

"The very one."

"No! Now I'm not referring to her, but you. How can you be so, so....?"

She searched unsuccessfully for the right word, but he stepped in to help:

"Cold...?"

"Cold isn't exactly right; I would say more indifferent, impassive, inscrutable, imperturbable... or even callous."

"What is a callous person, then, exactly?" Mauro Rivera asked with a barely imperceptible but unsettling smile playing on his lips. "Someone who doesn't have a soul, or who lost it along the way after having screwed over so many people?"

"What do I know? Only that you don't appear to have one."

"That may be correct, but for that reason alone, that maybe I don't have a soul, I suggest that after April fifteenth, you go back to Cuba and make it look like I died. You know well enough that I have eyes and ears everywhere and I wouldn't like to find out that you had become a threat to my security."

"Are you threatening me?"

"Does it sound like a threat?" he said, still smiling. "It all depends on you. If you want to stop being "Bigmouth" and enjoy your victory, which I've served up to you on a plate, for many years to come then, yes it is. Although I fear that if you do live for a long time you may eventually reach the conclusion that it wasn't a victory at all but more of a bitter defeat..."

Miami

On the fifteenth of April 1961, and with president Kennedy's blessing, a fleet of boats carrying a contingency made up of 1,200 men set sail from Port Cabeza in Nicaragua. Eight B26 aeroplanes bombed the military airports in Ciudad Libertad, San Antonio de los Baños and Santiago de Cuba, destroying a total of five planes: one Sea Fury, two B-26s and two cargo planes. The T-33 aeroplanes and Sea Fury fighters, however, remained intact. Castro's Sea Furies were faster than the B-26 planes that the invaders had. Brigade 2506 lost three bombers, but one of those carried on to the United States where the pilot claimed to be a deserter of the Cuban army seeking asylum, at the same time informing them that he and the other pilots had been behind the attack on the airports, a stunt that the Americans set up in order to hide their role in the operations being carried out there. This was the only bombing of the three planned, that actually went ahead.

Castro mobilized his troops ahead of a possible invasion. He also ordered house raids and large numbers of suspected opposition members were imprisoned.

After sailing for days and in the early hours of the morning, brigade 2506 landed on the Girón Beach escorted by their boats. They met with very little resistance. Some hours later, dozens of paratroopers were dropped from the air, inland, opening up the invaded zone with the aim of controlling all access roads to the area. During those early hours Cuban planes destroyed seven B-26s and put the Houston and Hidden River boats out of action so that all armaments destined to ground forces were lost. Fidel Castro's regular troops arrived gradually as reinforcements for the militias that had been trying to stave off the attack. By the end of the day the boats that belonged to the attacking brigade withdrew definitively without releasing ammunition or equipment. Fidel Castro realised that it was fundamental to attack these boats and therefore annihilate all supplies and the Revolution's Air Force achieved this objective.

The following day the counter-offensive began and the brigade's troops that were controlling access roads to the Girón beach were pushed back to the San Bals zone. The paratroops were forced to abandon their positions and head for the Girón beach in a bid to join up with other members of Brigade 2056. The revolutionary army took immediate control of the area. The attackers were forced to withdraw further and those that remained behind were forced to surrender in the early hours of the following morning. Accurate missile attacks and Castro's air fleet had ensured that ammunition was scarce on the beach and aerial support nonexistent. Kennedy's refusal to provide aerial cover for the Brigade was its final death sentence. The attackers began to flee, some looking for boats while others headed for cover in the swamps, although the majority were captured. The conflict was a resounding victory for the Cuban army.

Casualties exceeded one hundred on the attacking side; the amount of men captured was 1,189. The Cuban government militias suffered 176 casualties. Castro's prisoners were judged and condemned, although many of them were handed over to the United States in exchange for several million dollars. Towards the end of 1962 they started arriving in the US, where president Kennedy welcomed them as guests of honour.

The victory gave a boost to Fidel Castro's socialist revolution but deeply humiliated the US. Following an analysis of the defeat, Kennedy asked his brother to head up what became known as "Operation Mangosta". Its aim was to promote sabotage and other terrorist acts that would culminate in internal uprisings and the overthrowing of the regime, perhaps with a second invasion, but this time with direct US participation. One vital fact, however, stood in the way of the operation's objectives: "The Missile Crisis". After missile ramps were installed in Cuba by the USSR, tension between the two superpowers led to a real threat of nuclear war. The pact made between Kennedy and Kruschev, whereby the missiles were dismantled, was made on the basis that the US would not invade the island.

Diana "Bigmouth" would hear the words of the man who had served them their spectacular and indisputable victory "on a plate", ringing round her head every day until her death, as she read and re-read the dog-eared press cutting that told the story of the Battle of the Bay of Pigs.

As he had predicted, she no longer had any reason to feel proud of events described on that scrap of paper with its sordid bit of history printed on it.

Things had not progressed in the way that she had hoped they might. The freedom songs had turned into agony chants and the new hopes into old disappointments as it soon became all too clear that a fat, short and shaven tyrant had given up his seat to another bearded, tall and wiry tyrant.

As soon as she had made that realisation, she bitterly regretted having sucked off so many rancid cocks in the name of "The Revolution" that she had once so longed for.

Thanks to her sacrifices and the revolution's victory, her children were now dying of hunger, had suffered all kinds of injustices and dreamed only of escaping from the island, even if it meant being eaten by sharks along the way. They cursed the hideous traitor who had caused the opposition to lose the Bay of Pigs battle. There is nothing worse than the dreams of youth turning into the bitter nightmares of old age.

California, 2007

"Why do you look so worried?"

The old lady was taking breakfast in the garden by the pool as usual, enjoying the beautiful garden and the huge ocean that stretched beyond it. She put the newspaper that she had been reading to one side and stirred some sugar into her coffee thoughtfully.

"I'm surprised by the fact that despite the murder of five of Dall&Houston's main shareholders by this mysterious terrorist that is threatening to kill them all, its share price on the stock exchange hasn't fallen at all."

"I don't understand much about stock quotes."

"Nobody understands my dear. Nobody! The crashes sparked by the mortgage chaos the world over demonstrates that the supposed Wall Street 'experts' are a bunch of fools that have no idea about what is going to happen unless it's something they started themselves. But this, when about twenty per cent of this awful company belongs to speculators, but prices remain unchanged as if nothing had happened, unsettles me."

"Please explain it to me more clearly," Salka Embarek beseeched. "Do I have to remind you again that I'm just a poor terrorist student on strike."

"Don't make out you are stupid when you are not, but I will try all the same," she replied, spreading her toast with strawberry jam. "If you were the heir to a substantial amount of shares from someone who had been killed because he had been a significant shareholder in that company, it is only common sense that you would try and get rid of the shares as soon as possible so as to not get mixed up in something that smacks of blood and corruption, wouldn't you?"

"I suppose so."

"Well that's my point of view, which should mean that right

now millions of Dall&Houston shares should be up for sale, but that doesn't seem to be the case here. Something's going on which has essentially removed them from speculation."

The old woman chewed on some toast, before adding, "If there's one thing in this world that catches my attention it's a mystery."

"Wasting time over trying to solve mysteries far a field is a rich man's preoccupation," the girl replied disconcertingly, while tucking into a hearty breakfast of fried eggs and ham. "I suppose the rest of us mere mortals just have to get on with resolving the mystery of our monthly bills."

"Have you ever had to pay any bills in your life?"

"None. But I have a hefty bill for whoever it was that took away everything I once had."

"Well it's exactly these guys, darling. These very ones! Dall&Houston is the corporation that was guilty of the war that killed your family and although it is of some comfort to know that they are paying for it with their lives, or walking around in fear of them, I would still love to know what's really happening here."

"But what would you get out of knowing?" she persisted.

"I would satisfy my curiosity and add fuel to one of the few fires that must never go out, whatever our age: the capacity to reason and find sense in everything that appears senseless."

"Can't you just be happy with solving the crossword or the chess problems in the paper?"

"More respect child!" the old lady remonstrated, but in good humour. "I am trying to teach you how to live and above all how to think, but instead you insist on annoying me. At this rate you'll send me to the grave in the belief that I'm leaving all this, that has cost me so much to get, to someone who won't have a clue what to do with it…"

"And I insist that I don't want you to leave me anything, replied the girl sincerely. "It's true that I wouldn't know what to do with it and from the way you behave, it might be better that I never find out how you got it all anyway. Maybe you don't believe me, but after everything that's happened I'd prefer to reach old age with a clear conscience."

"It's expensive to keep a clear conscience dear; very expensive. If you don't have enough money to start with, sooner or later you'll end up getting your hands dirty and your so-called conscience! I know from experience," Mary Lacombe said in a voice that had suddenly taken on a more serious tone.

The girl remained silent, hoping that the moment had come for her to reveal all, but the old lady managed to elude the subject once again, saying, "I admit that I have done too many things that I shouldn't have and only a few that I should have; and I confess that if I am to make you into the only friend that I have or ever will have, then I have to be totally honest with you, but I still don't feel quite ready to do that."

-There isn't any prep work to be done if you're planning on telling the truth. The truth, after all is the truth, end of story," Salka reasoned. "But lies need careful preparation, because the options are endless and you will always run the risk of choosing the wrong one."

"I need time because I'm afraid that when you find out you'll leave me."

"Is it that bad?"

"Worse than you could ever imagine."

"I can't imagine anything worse than the horrible things I've seen. Starting with the pieces of my mother that I found scattered around the garden of our house and ending with a bomb being strapped to my body, which could have been detonated at any moment. Compared with the anguish and desperation that I felt after they'd converted me in to an aspiring suicide bomber, any story you end up telling me will be like a fairytale."

"You have a point. At the end of the day I was always aware of what I was doing and entirely in possession of my wits, while the things that happened to you, well, they happened without you going out to look for them and you were only a child."

The old lady moved forward and took the girl's hands in her own as she whispered beseechingly, "Allow me a little more time please!"

"You've had enough time!" she retorted angrily. "I warned you that if I ended up feeling like you too were manipulating me, I'd probably shoot you and I'm starting to suspect that you keeping me here, living like a queen in this enormous palace, with a swimming pool and six people at my beck and call, is just another form of manipulation. I don't want to get used to a life like this, without knowing why it is being offered to me, so you'd better start thinking about when it is that you're going to tell me what you're hiding, or one of these days I'll walk out that door and I'm not sure you'll ever see me again. You might like mysteries, but I don't."

Nicaragua, 1961

When they met in Nicaragua, Mauro Rivero convinced the Cubans setting off for the Bay of Pigs that he should travel with the mercenaries contracted by the CIA, as they would need an interpreter they could trust. That same day he convinced the CIA recruits that he should sail and disembark with his own compatriots since he would prefer to be with men of his own blood if things got nasty.

Mauro Rivero did not, in fact, board any boat, but remained on land under cover of darkness, looking out to sea until the lights of the boats were no longer visible as they sailed northeast, just before the dawn of that spring day in 1963, a date in Cuban history that many have since mourned. Then, with the first light of day, he disappeared in to the thick swampy inland that bordered the so-called Mosquito Coast.

No one ever saw him again.

At least, not as the person known as Mauro Rivero.

Officially, the body of Mauro Rivero Elgosa was taken to his mother by the Cuban authorities and laid to rest in the forgotten cemetery of a small town on the Florida peninsula, not far from Tampa.

Nobody put flowers on his grave and a few years later even the tombstone, which marked a Christian burial, disappeared.

The fortune he had amassed over many years from both his legal and illegal businesses, disappeared shortly before he left for Nicaragua, along with the commissions that he had received, together with the CIA agents, for the purchase of arms and supplies that had been destined for the unlucky 2056 Brigade.

It would be fair to say that Mauro Rivero was the only exile who had actually benefited from the failed invasion of Cuba.

Almost five million dollars in the early seventies.

Almost five million dollars and six American passports that a corrupt member of the Central Intelligence Agency had sorted out for him, in exchange for him keeping an eye on a certain shipment of arms that was destined to members of an expedition, but which never actually reached its intended destination.

From Nicaragua, Mauro Rivero travelled to Brazil where he underwent cosmetic surgery, and with a photo of his new face in his passport along with a set of new personal details, he set up home in an old colonial house in San Diego, convinced that the warm climate in southern California would help to keep his strange illness at bay.

He was just thirty years old. He was still a virgin. This was due to the basic fact that he had never been attracted to a woman, let alone a man.

For the man that these days called himself Mark Stevens, sexual relations were senseless and unappealing.

Maybe an erection was out of the question due to the fragility of his capillary vessels, which might have impeded the flow of blood to his penis, but physical speculation aside, the truth was that mentally he had never felt the urge to so much as touch another human being.

He was who he was and that for him was enough.

In some ways he was more like a sphinx than a human being.

A sphinx who took great satisfaction in knowing that he had successfully outwitted everyone, beginning with the stupid conspirators that made up the so-called White Rose group, to the all-powerful cretins at the FBI and CIA and ending with his partners at the previously feared and revered Corporation.

They had all been deceived into believing that he was dead.

The Corporation! How he missed it.

For about four months now he had spent his time reading for hours on end by the sea, going to the cinema or eating at some of the best restaurants along the coast, always alone, which had given him enough time to reflect and conclude that it was time he created another Corporation; a Corporation that this time would be a much more powerful, impregnable and sophisticated entity. The three factors he deemed essential in order for the project to move ahead successfully, were: economic means, a wealth of experience and a total absence of any kind of scruples.

Perhaps the only redeeming feature of Mauro Rivero's moral make-up was that, just as he was unable to tell the difference between the skin of a beautiful woman and a lorry driver; or distinguish between the aromatic note of a cognac and a common rat poison; or tell the difference between an excellent Havana cigar or a menthol cigarette; he was completely incapable of making a distinction between good and evil.

Everything that benefited him personally was good.

Anything that damaged him personally was bad.

He only had to make sure he followed those simple rules unswervingly, in order to ensure that he never put a foot wrong.

So, after some serious thought as to how he should go about creating another "Corporation", one that was much more powerful than before and with different collaborators, he upped and left for Los Angeles, found a public telephone booth and dialled for Miami.

When the phone was picked up at the other end he spoke with a deep and raspy voice with no trace of an accent, one that he had practiced many times alone, but had not really used otherwise, apart from on the odd occasion:

"Lee? Lee Kitanen?"

"That's me..." the man on the other end of the line answered, "Who's calling?"

"My name is irrelevant..." he replied with his usual studied calm. "What does matter is that I have in my possession receipts signed by you for two shipments of assault rifles, pistols, hand grenades and ammunition provided by the South Panama commando unit, and destined for the late 2056 Brigade.

"Only half of it arrived at its destination and I also have in my possession your Swiss bank account details as well as the date on which the Colombian guerrillas put three hundred and seventy thousand dollars into it, as payment for those missing weapons."

There was a long, drawn out silence, which Mauro Rivero had been expecting, given the disagreeable and sudden nature of the news that he had just imparted.

"Are you trying to blackmail me?" he finally asked.

"Of course!"

"And do you know who I am?"

"Of course!" the Cuban admitted. "That's why I'm calling, because you've been promoted to Area Manager, which means you are on your way to becoming one of the Agency's top dogs. Neither of us would want this information to become public. You won't be of much use to me in prison."

"I'm warning you that I won't do anything that goes against the interests of my country," Lee Kitanen said sharply. "I'd rather spend a few years in the shade for corruption than risk execution for being a traitor."

"I'm not a traitor either, don't worry," Mauro Rivero said, trying to appease him. "Politics is neither here nor there to me. This is about business, only business, and I can guarantee you that in one year that three hundred and seventy thousand dollars will seem like the tip of an iceberg."

"I don't do drug trafficking."

"Nor do I."

"In that case, what is this all about?"

"You'll see. But in the mean time, all I need are your contacts with the Colombian guerrillas. If that information works then you'll get one hundred thousand dollars put into your Swiss bank account. If not you'll get a bullet in the head the minute you leave little Nancy's apartment. Out of curiosity... do you still water ski opposite the Hotel Delmónico?"

"Who the hell are you and how come you know so much about me?"

"I'm you're new business partner, mate. Your new partner."

Texas

The president of Brazil, Lula da Silva, who has always been seemingly opposed to privatization, has given the go ahead for part of the Brazilian jungle to be privatised on the back of strong evidence that claims current attempts to preserve the Amazon are becoming increasingly futile.

He said that the decision to move ahead and lease out the land was due to an increase in illegal deforestation. The Government hopes that if companies exploit the wood or other products in a sustainable manner, it would discourage illegal deforestation.

The first area to be passed over to private management is 90,000 hectares in size, part of the National Grove in the Jamari Reserve in the state of Rondonia, which covers a total of 220,000 hectares.

The land will be up for bidding and the three winning companies will be able to exploit the low jungle plains as long as they meet with certain conditions. The first plot to come up for tender will be made up of three lots of 45,000, 30,000 and 15,000 hectares each. These lots can only be exploited by Brazilian companies, irrespective of the origin of their capital and they will sign contracts of between five and forty years.

The private companies that win the tender will be obliged to carry out the reforestation of areas previously devastated by fire. The amount of trees that can be felled per hectare in each area for commercial use will be regulated.

According to Government sources, both the financial and technological aspects of the offers will be assessed, but priority will be given to the latter. Therefore, it is not guaranteed that the biggest financial offer will win the tender as greater consideration will be given to the one with the strongest technological criteria, which would ensure greater operational efficiency and therefore have stronger social and environmental benefits.

Of the Amazon jungle's 194 million hectares, currently the property of the Brazilian state, one million hectares are slated for privatization.

"It's almost under wraps and the biggest lot, the forty-five thousand hectare one, which is the one we're interested in, should be ours…" Peter Corkenham began, and after making sure that everyone at the meeting had read through the press cutting he had just given them, he continued:

"Nobody will be able to come anywhere near what we've offered in economic terms and nobody will guarantee on paper that no more than five of every one hundred trees will be felled, whilst trees are simultaneously replanted in another twenty deforested areas of the Amazon basin. We have also guaranteed that we will respect the local indigenous tribes and fauna."

"And no one thinks your generosity a little odd?" Tony Walker enquired.

"No. Because we've convinced our government to substantially increase the tax exemptions for investments connected with environmental issues. If we go about this intelligently then the changing climate could actually be our Trojan Horse that opens up many more gates.

"In fact, it is doing just that in many parts of the world already," the ever-incisive Jeff Hamilton pointed out. "Certain media forms are provoking a kind of collective hysteria like the ones we saw in the fifties with nuclear war or in the seventies during the petrol crisis."

"For good or for bad, human beings behave like pendulums. For almost two centuries now we've unwittingly gone about destroying nature and now we're in a sudden hurry to pick up all the pieces," the Dall&Houston president noted.

"What we have to do is clean up our image and become an example, starting with the extraction of coltan, which we will endeavour to do without damaging the immediate environment."

"And what kind of work force will you employ?" Judy Slander ventured, a member who was so shy that every time he spoke he sounded like he was making an apology for daring to interrupt. "Children, like in the Congo?"

"Absolutely not!" Hamilton reassured him. "We'll employ adults, protected by Brazilian laws who'll have all the work safety guarantees that they'd have in civilized countries."

"Won't that put the price of the product up too much?"

"We could put coltan on the market for a half of what it currently goes for and we'd still earn millions because in less than three years we'll have a monopoly on the market."

"That is all very well..." Slander ventured timidly and then gesturing to the empty seats, said, "It all sounds like a wonderful future if we're alive to enjoy it, but you can't ignore the fact that every time we meet there is one less person around this table."

"I think we've found a place where we will all be safe until the Al Rashid problem is resolved," Peter Corkenham said confidently.

"And that is?"

"On my ranch. The Blackwaters are turning it into an impenetrable fortress and by next week we'll have lodgings for all of you, including your families for those of you who wish to bring them.

"My children have to go to school."

"Probably better that they remain out of college for the moment than without a father. In my case I won't be leaving Seven Oaks until I feel absolutely sure there's no risk involved. Everyone else will be free to move around of course, but on your heads be it."

***

"I can't take any more risks. I've done everything you asked me to do without questioning your orders. I've accepted that my friends, including my own family despise me for being one of the main perpetrators behind this unjust war, but I swear to you that I've reached my limit."

"I understand."

"Your understanding is not enough sir," the slight man muttered, clearly overwhelmed by recent events. "For four years I've played the role of spectator without scruples and I admit that you have repaid me generously, but you have to understand that my life and the future of my children are now at stake. What will they do when I'm dead and they discover that I'm an impostor, that I don't even have one measly share in Dall&Houston and that I've left them in ruins?

The man in the black hood sat down on the other side of the table, drumming his fingers on it as usual, meditated for a little while, nodded and then in his characteristically deep and raspy voice said:

"You're right and the risk is excessive. But I still need to have someone on the inside of the board of directors to keep me up to date with what those scheming bastards are up to, especially all that stuff they're planning to do with coltan. I hate to imagine what would happen if Dall&Houston manage to monopolize the market with a metal that is of such strategic importance. I've worked with them for years, I've carried out endless amounts of dirty work for them and I know their tricks and the limits they will go to get what they want."

"But why do you want to know all this, when, like you said, you've spent so much time collaborating with them?"

"For that reason alone! Because I've collaborated with them and one of my greatest pleasures is proving to myself that I can also deceive them. I love deceiving anyone who thinks they're that clever! It makes me sick to think that the second most important man in our country, is at the same time the most corrupt, and I can't bear the idea that one day, between them and American Mineral Fields, owned by George Bush's father, they'll bring the world and the devil himself to their knees, in order to control this accursed coltan."

"I understand your reasons sir, but what has that got to do with any of this? I've been your puppet so far, but now my head's got a price on it. What am I supposed to do?"

The hooded man sat there once again lost in reflection, drumming his fingers on the table, before enquiring:

"Would it make things any easier if I put an insurance policy in your wife and children's name to the value of fifty million dollars?"

"An insurance policy of fifty million dollars?" the small man repeated, both surprised and a little disconcerted. "Are you serious?"

"Very serious. Ten million in your hand and a life insurance of fifty. Are you interested?"

"Of course!"

"In that case gather your family together and take refuge at Corkenham's ranch, and pray that those animals in dark glasses carrying machine guns, manage to keep you alive. You'll have the money in your bank tomorrow and the only thing you have to do now is take your lap top with you and keep me up to date with everything that's going on."

California - Amazon

When Mary Lacombe suggested to Salka Embarek that "they go fish some enormous fish" the girl thought that she was planning to take her out in a private yacht, but the old lady positively balked at the very suggestion.

"Good God no! The sea terrifies me and I hardly know how to swim and when the boat starts rocking I'm the first to throw up."

"So where then?"

"I mean river fish."

"Salmon from Alaska?"

"Maybe you think I'd like to die of cold? And anyway, the salmons are barely bigger than trout there. I'm talking "huge fish", almost five meters long and two hundred kilos in weight; the famous pirarucu found in the Amazon."

"Are you really asking me if I want to go and fish in the river Amazon?" the Iraqi enquired, hardly able to believe her ears. "Are you mad?"

"Mad for what?" the old lady said surprised. "All you need to go fishing in the Amazon is a passion for it and loads of money, both of which I have in abundance. Can you imagine what it must be like to fight with a pirarucu that weighs two tonnes?"

"And what if it's a piranha?"

"We'll eat it."

"I thought it was the piranhas that ate people, not people who ate piranhas."

"We are different, apart from the fact that piranhas are usually small…" she paused, narrowing one eye slyly and said:

"Besides, my story deserves to be told by the light of an open fire in a camping spot on the shores of a jungle river."

"You're getting crazier by the day."

"Maybe it's Alzheimer's, but I don't want to die without ever having had an adventure in the jungle, and if I don't do it soon you'll have to take me in a wheelchair, which would be quite impractical with all those trees, roots and liana around the place."

"Have you always been like this?" Salka Embarek asked. "So unpredictable and strange?"

"No darling, no," came her quick and honest response. "For most of my life I've been far too level headed and proud of being able to control by emotions under any circumstances. With age, however, I have learnt that this kind of behaviour might make you a lot of money, but brings with it solitude, sadness and bitterness. The time has come for me to change."

"But to go from a river in the Mid-West to one in the Amazon is quite a big change."

"We shall see!"

It had to be said that when Mary Lacombe took the decision to do something, she meant it. Only forty-eight hours later, her luxury private jet was ready for them at the Los Angeles airport, waiting to take the two women, the pilots and one air hostess, first to Guayaquil in Ecuador and from there directly to Porto Velho, capital of the Rondonia state in the middle of the Amazon jungle.

At the end of the runway, two off-road vehicles were waiting for them accompanied by four heavily armed body guards who drove them to an enormous mansion that had its own private jetty, swimming pool, tennis courts, luxuriant gardens, trees filled with macaws and an esplanade with a helicopter on it.

It looked like it must have belonged to one of the mythical "Gaucho Kings"; a kind of medieval castle that had been exquisitely restored.

The girl could not believe her eyes.

"And all this excess...?" She enquired even more perplexed than ever. "However many fish we catch, they're still going to cost us twenty thousand dollars a kilo..."

"So what? Or maybe you don't fancy travelling round the

world's most impenetrable jungle by helicopter? From what I've been told, if you cross the river and head off into those trees you don't come back."

"Who would have thought so looking at this city, these cars and above all this house...!"

"Never trust appearances little one, never! Rondonia is as big as half of Iraq or half of California, and Porto Velho is practically the only place that you could call 'civilized' in the entire state. There are two thousand kilometres of straight jungle between here and Brazilia, almost a thousand kilometres of jungle to Manaus, and a little more to Iquitos in Peru. That is to say we're in the heart of the "Green Inferno". This city full of billboards, bright lights and cars has a reputation of being the most hideous, seedy settlement ever to have been created by man."

The old woman had a point. Porto Velho used to go by the name of San Antonio which just a century ago was one of the most feared and reviled cities on earth, a place where blood, death, cruelty and suffering had reigned.

The city was situated on the shores of the immense Madeira river, which, just a few kilometres down stream turned in to a terrifying and roaring cacophony of nineteen angry rapids and impressive waterfalls that joined together to form possibly the most impenetrable wall that nature had ever created to curb the advances of civilisation.

It was difficult to imagine that anyone would have ever have dared to challenge this furious wall of water at the foothills of the Andean mountain ranges, but higher up, huge woods of Heveas brasiliensis had been discovered, woods where every single tree dripped with a white resin that in those days was worth its weight in gold.

Rubber!

Towards the end of the eighteen hundreds these rubber trees were practically crying with gold. The woods full of heveas could have made hundreds, thousands of explorers rich, but they remained untouched and of no use to anyone simply because on the one side you were met with sheer mountains, some five thousand meters tall, and on the other side, the Madeira waterfalls, on whose edges, as if that were not enough, lived tribes of cannibals.

Hundreds of ambitious Brazilian rubber collectors, known as the siringueiros, had tried to reach the fabulous treasure by climbing up from the edges of the rivers, but mostly ended up being devoured by savages, so that the rubber remained there, untouched by human hand.

Bolivian rubber workers would spend months scouring the area for routes through and around the mountain ranges, but rarely made it back, because even if the convoys, weighed down with their heavy loads, made it back to the inhospitable mountain ranges they were usually met with equally hostile tribes that would make sure only one man in every twenty managed to get back to civilisation and only then with a tenth of the initial load.

It is a well known adage that says human ambition knows no boundaries, and one cursed day in 1854 somebody came up with the disastrous idea of building a railway through four hundred kilometres of thick and swampy jungle from the miniscule enclave of San Antonio, to the shores of the Madeira and on to one of its tributaries, the Mamoré, which snaked up above the waterfalls and on whose shores the rubber trees were said to grow like mushrooms.

An English company was contracted to build the city and start work on the railway, but after thousands of workers were killed by arrows and darts poisoned with "curare" that the savages released from deep within the vegetation, or died from fevers, snakebites and fierce animals, the company withdrew.

Years later, an American company based in Philadelphia started up the work again, but after losing a third of its workers, having only managed to lay the first six kilometres of track and having invested thirty tonnes of gold, it too was forced to withdraw. Of the seven hundred Germans that had been contracted specifically from Europe, the fifty that remained decided to flee down stream. Only six of them managed to reach Manaus, the nearest civilised place.

Another American company, this time from Maine, took up the work and after calculating that each kilometre of track would cost them fifty lives, that is to say a body every twenty meters, they went about importing a workforce by enslaving as many natives, men, women and children, as they could from the jungle area close by.

After fifty years of corrupt work, the Madeira-Mamoré railway was finished in October 1912, and along its four hundred kilometres you can still see the markings that represent the thousands of nameless graves bearing the sole inscription: "Killed by the Indians".

The most tragic twist to this disastrous story, and perhaps at the same time comic, is that one year later an English explorer managed to get hold of a sack of seeds from the Amazon, despite it being a heinous crime and punishable by death in those days, and soon after Africa and Indonesia were growing huge crops of heveas brasiliensis so cheaply that the "Train of Death" never actually operated. In the heart of Porto Velho, on the shores of the river, you can still visit the small station, now a painful relic of the past.

A few days after their arrival, the two women decided to take the old locomotive that pulled two crumbling old carriages behind it, on the thirty kilometre journey it sometimes made into the jungle, in memory of what to this day must have been the most bloody, costly and useless project that human beings, in peaceful times, have ever been known to embark on.

Malibu

It took Lee Kitanen eight months to reach the conclusion that it would be much more lucrative, comfortable and safe to work with someone he did not know, other than by his deep voice, particularly someone who had him "strung up by the balls", being in possession of information that could put him in prison, than continue in his job as a special agent that afforded him a meagre salary and paltry retirement rights.

So, following instructions, he moved to the West Coast and dedicated himself to "subcontracting", by telephone and without ever revealing his identity, all of the most professional criminals that he knew of, having worked at the Central Intelligence Agency for so many years and having spent a lot of time searching through the archives, prior to taking definitive sick leave.

To ensure that he was given sick leave he spent one month downing as much vinegar as he could, which gave him such a skeletal, washed out appearance that the doctors were convinced that the poor man had one foot in the grave, although they were unable to diagnose his unfortunate condition.

And so, when he told them that all he wanted to do was to spend the rest of his days in his native Colorado he was let go without question.

"Maybe the mountain air will do you good…" they told him sceptically. "Just maybe!"

They would never have guessed that Lee Kitanen had in fact eschewed the Colorado air for a more luxurious lifestyle in Malibu where he made a swift and full recovery.

He loved his extravagant house on the beach, the beautiful girls that visited him regularly and the abundance of money he now had. He felt extraordinarily good knowing that he was part of an organisation so cleverly structured that it emanated a marvellous aroma of impunity, whatever hideous crime was being committed at whatever time of day.

He did not have the vaguest idea who his boss was, his subordinates had no idea who he was and their subordinates likewise.

They did not operate like a Mafia group or a bunch of organized criminals in the traditional sense, since the only communication they had was via laptops, mobile phones, bank transfers, and packets picked up in the left-luggage offices at airports around the world.

Every single "job" was masterminded by the Boss – or Mariel – with pinpoint accuracy, which meant that Lee Kitanen had very little thinking to do, he just had to ensure that, once the mechanics were in place, everything moved ahead like clockwork. And if anybody slipped up he would make sure that they were not around to make the same mistake twice.

Mariel was incredibly generous to his faithful subordinates, but cruel and unforgiving to anyone who did not follow his orders to the letter.

The methods they used to dispatch orders became increasingly more sophisticated over the years, and more complex with every new technological advance made, until it became possible to send instructions that were totally indecipherable to anyone who did not have the exact system of interpretation to hand.

The system's invention was of course the brainchild of Mariel's twisted mind. First of all he would type the whole text of a message into the computer, however long, in a perfectly legible way and without any kind of code. He would select one of every twelve words in the text and leave a gap in the place that they were originally in, then send the riddle to a fixed e-mail address. He then isolated a second group of words in the same way, always one in every twelve, which would be sent to another e-mail address, usually in a different country. By repeating that same operation twelve times over, the message could circulate freely, but in fragments, on the internet. Only the group's members had the access codes to a handful of fixed email addresses, which represented just a few of all the billions of fixed addresses that already existed out there on the web. By accessing these addresses they were able to gather together their instructions by printing the different messages back on to the same piece of paper, which saw the whole text come together once again.

Nobody has ever managed to make an estimate, not even a close one, of the hundreds of millions of messages that circulate daily on the internet, which means that finding twelve of them, isolating them and putting them together, would have been virtually impossible, unless you knew what you were looking for in the first place.

Mariel also made sure that he used between eight and ten different computers when sending the messages. The levels of impunity that he worked to achieve meant that nobody ever met anybody, even though they worked as a team. And that combined with his complete lack of scruples regarding the kind of dirty work he carried out, meant that in the course of just over thirty years, the new "Corporation" created by Mauro Rivero, had become the most lucrative, criminal and respected criminal organisation in the entire country.

Texas

The enormous Seven Oaks ranch, some two hundred kilometres west of Houston, was a famous slice of paradise, with its own private runway, dense woodland, winding streams, verdant prairies where cows and horse grazed, still lakes and an eighteen hole golf course, of which its owner was especially proud.

For a week now the place had been converted into an impregnable fortress. Two helicopters constantly hovered over the place, which was patrolled on land by dozens of lorries full of armed men and kept watch over day and night from two high towers that had been installed on top of the hills, facing west, the only place from which you could access the ranch without being spotted from some distance away.

The spectacular guest house, put up in record time, was also protected by an electric fence and a dozen dogs trained to kill, who could detect the presence of anyone that they had not been presented to or smelled before hand.

The place was, without doubt, a golden cage where no one lacked for anything and from where business could be conducted as usual from its spacious office that had all the latest and necessary technology available.

But still, to all intents and purposes, it was a cage.

Eight of the surviving members of the Dall&Houston board of directors had accepted the selfless hospitality of their president, while the others had opted to disappear momentarily in the hope that the feared and reviled Aarohum Al Rashid would not be able to find them.

From the outside it might have looked like the guests staying at Seven Oaks were enjoying a fabulous vacation, were it not for the fact that nobody dared to play golf or swim in the pool, or sit out under the starry Texan skies on those the warm nights, but remained huddled inside and under cover.

But despite all of the security measures in place and the permanent presence of the sour-faced Blackwaters security men, hired personally by Jeff Hamilton, it was fear, not Peter Corkenham, that ruled those uncomfortable days at Seven Oaks.

Not even three weeks had passed, when one afternoon a small plane landed on the ranch's runway and an agitated Tony Walker got out and asked the president to gather all of the board members together immediately.

"Why?"

"I've promised Mariel that I wouldn't say a word until we are all together."

"Not even to me?"

"Not even to you. You know how it is. The walls have ears and don't think I'm betraying your confidence, it's just that I don't want to ruin what chance of salvation you might have."

"It's that important, what you have to say?"

"I think so."

Reluctantly and visibly annoyed by not knowing in advance what the meeting was about, the Dall&Houston president managed to get all eight guests together in his office.

Tony Walker got straight to the point.

"Mariel called me to tell me that he has managed to find out who is carrying out Al Rashid's orders. He believes he is in a position to catch them, and maybe, and I mean a big maybe, they will lead him to the one that's giving out the orders and financing them."

"So why hasn't he done that already?"

"He thinks that it might mean a confrontation with some very dangerous groups, which could unleash a war of unpredictable consequences. And a costly one at that; very costly."

"I don't think there is anything more costly than our own lives..." Judy Slander ventured timidly.

"I agree there..." Ed Pierce said. "How much does he want now?"

"Three hundred million."

"Three hundred million!" Peter Corkenham spluttered, in shock. "Has he gone mad?"

"Not at all! He gave me the impression that he was very relaxed and was not overly excited by your offer in the first place. As far as I can tell he's enjoying his retirement."

"Well as far as I'm concerned, he can go on enjoying his retirement."

"This is a decision we have to take together," intervened Ed Pierce. "If there is the slightest chance, remote though it may be, that we don't have to spend the rest of our lives imprisoned in these four walls, we need to take a look at it... Or not?"

There was a murmur of acceptance, which forced the president to intervene once again and ask, "What guarantee of success can he offer?"

"For the minute just to liquidate the liquidators," Tony Walker said.

"That's it?"

"You have to trust that by doing just that he'll find a way of getting to that son of a bitch, which seems to me quite sensible."

"And if he doesn't manage that?"

"In that case, two things could happen," Tony Walker continued in a grave tone of voice. "That Al Rashid decides to stop in his tracks as we get closer to him and he senses danger, or it takes some time for him to reorganize himself, which would also give us a breather; something which everyone needs, by the looks of things."

"A breath is just a breath..." muttered an increasingly disgruntled Hamilton.

"When you're up to your neck in water, a breath might just be the thing that saves you..." noted Judy Slander. "This Mariel guy seems to be a lot cleverer than the rest, given that so far neither the police, nor the FBI, nor the CIA nor the Chihuahua Breeding Association or the Yellow Carnation Group, have given us any inkling of hope that they are in any way on the right track. He, whoever "he" is, does seem to be on the right scent, and to be honest as the situation stands, I'm ready to cling on to the last hope we have."

"And me!"

"I'm with you there!"

"One moment!" begged Jeff Hamilton, standing up and holding up his arms as if trying to bring some order to the meeting, "What the hell is going on and what are you all talking about? Mariel, who as we well know, is a son of a bitch without scruples, who will sell out to the highest bidder and betray whoever takes his fancy, can only tell us that he has located the people that work for Al Rashid and can get rid of them. But he has failed to give us any proof of this, not even one name," he shook his head in disbelief as if he still could not believe the situation. "Do you really believe him and accept those terms without any other guarantees?" he asked. "He's taking us for a ride! Pretending to retire definitively, but not before taking three hundred million dollars. Christ! What a bunch of madmen you are, or even better, cowards!"

An embarrassing silence followed, during which time they all looked at each other, some ashamed, others intimidated, so that Tony Walker had to step in once again, this time with some even more worrying news:

"He said that if it came to this, and as far as I can tell, it has done, I should tell you something that he would rather have kept secret, so as not to worry you any more than you already are..." he paused, giving a melodramatic edge to what he was about to say, before adding, "He is convinced that you will find that some of the Blackwaters working on the ranch, or at least one of them, is working for Al Rashid!"

"It's not possible!"

"Everything is possible my friend. Remember they are merce-naries and mercenaries by definition sell out to the highest bidder," he said turning to Peter Corkenham. "How much do those killers charge to risk their lives protecting you?" he asked.

"About fifteen thousand dollars a month on average, but they've assured me that they are all totally trustworthy."

"Mariel assures me that Al Rashid has put a price of two million dollars on each of your heads, so add up the difference and you decide whether they're on your side."

"So basically we're more at risk locked up in that house than we would be out there on our own?" the increasingly distraught Judy Slander said.

"It would seem that way."

"God help us then."

"Right! I suggest we take a break to reflect on the situation more calmly and tomorrow we will meet again and make a decision one way or another."

San Diego

It was not until the mid-eighties, a long time after his mother had died and been cremated, and after the body that had been buried in the small cemetery under the name of "Mauro Rivero" was removed by "somebody" and the scant remains placed in to a mass grave, that the real Mauro Rivero felt completely safe in his comfortable, colonial house in San Diego

This new-found sense of security, however, was short-lived as news soon reached him that a group of survivors from the failed Bay of Pigs invasion, who were convinced that Mauro Rivero had *not* actually died, and that he was responsible for their doomed attack, having sold their information to the Castro revolutionaries, were looking to settle the score, whatever it may take.

The amount that they were offering for any information on him was proof enough that they were serious.

The plastic surgery had, he was certain, changed his features to the extent that not even his oldest friends would recognize him, but he was also certain that, were any one of those "friends" made an attractive enough offer, they would assist in the search for clues that might eventually lead to him.

Every single one of his old buddies from the Corporation knew that he suffered from a strange and uncommon disease, so it was quite probable that there were already dozens of Cuban exiles out there looking for a tall, dark man of about fifty odd years who suffered from an extreme form of this so-called "Raynaud Syndrome".

Forever this accursed illness! Forever suffering for as long as he could remember. Forever persecuting him wherever he was.

It was the cross that had been forced to bear day after day, that limited his movements, that meant he could not use air conditioning or travel in commercial aeroplanes to far away places that he would have loved to visit.

His condition was the true Achilles heel of someone who had spent his entire life, often by methods that would be considered totally inhumane, trying to build a wall around himself that was as impregnable as was humanly possible.

So much wasted effort!

It had taken him half a century to build this fortress around himself and now he had to face up to the fact that its very foundations were crumbling. This man who had spent half a century in virtual solitude, always in tough combat with the outside world in defence of his sacred privacy, who wore an armour that no one had ever managed to penetrate, was now faced with the harsh reality that he was suddenly more vulnerable than the guy next door.

He knew well enough that over the years Cuban exiles had penetrated every corner of North American society and in every city and every village you would meet Cubans who were fiercely opposed to the Castro regime and who would not only be honoured, but take great personal satisfaction in finding out the whereabouts of the man who was so directly responsible for the fact that the island's cruel dictator had remained in power.

Mauro Rivero had not spoken one word of Spanish for years. He never read a book or a paper in his paternal language or listened to the radio or flicked over to a Mexican channel on television, of which there were many in southern California, in a mighty effort to completely cut off his roots.

This was, however, a slightly futile endeavour, since his real roots lay in a town in central France, where some of his ancestors, no one knows why, had also suffered from this inconsiderate illness.

It was like trying to pretend that the skin of a Senegalese descendent was no longer dark or that the eyes of a Japanese child had become rounded, just because they had lived in California for the greater part of their lives.

If his ancestors had been Senegalese or his mother had been Japanese, the Californian air alone would never have been enough to erase those genetic traits.

Neither was it enough to keep his blood flowing normally and his hands from going blue whenever the temperature dropped.

He focused his attention on trying to silence all the doctors, hospitals, clinics and even witch doctors that he had consulted during his stay on the West Coast in his search to find some relief from his symptoms. He soon realized, however, that he would never be able to stop them all from talking, least of all erase the tracks that he had left along the way. The survivors of the one thousand five hundred members of the 2056 Brigade that he had sent headlong into defeat, way back on that decisive day of March fifteenth, would sooner or later find him. They would search him out to the end and then hang him from a lamppost, having tortured him to death first.

He did not blame them. From his point of view they had every right to be looking for him, to capture him, to remove his eyes and skin him alive.

He would have done the same for much less, and even though he was a totally cold, immoral man, it did not stop him from recognizing that justice was justice.

His debts to the rest of mankind were without doubt so excessive that there was no way he could ever pay any of it back. The only thing he could do in his defence was to try and prevent them from even coming to look for that repayment.

So the day that he found out that a group of private detectives were on the trail of a man who lived in southern California and who suffered from an uncommon illness known as the "Raynaud Syndrome", he set fire to his comfortable home in San Diego, making sure that it burnt down to the very foundations.

He watched from a distance as his past went up in flames, then turned away and disappeared into the night.

Amazon

She could not sleep.

The old lady, exhausted by the long journey had gone to bed early, but Salka Embarek, overcome by so many different emotions, being on the shores of this mysterious river in the middle of such a wild world, listening to the strange songs of the nocturnal birds that lived in the treetops towering high above the terrace of her bedroom, was far too excited to close her eyes.

It was the smell of the jungle that surprised her above all. It was a dense and humid smell, punctuated by a thousand scents that bore no relation to anything she had ever experienced before, not even in the Green Zone of the market in Baghdad, where you could find an incredible variety of flowers and greenery.

It was not just the smell of the different flowers and species, but of the trees, of their very essence, which, alongside the sweat of the beasts that lived there, had permeated the river for thousands of kilometres and which the breeze now carried to the girl sitting at its shores.

The air was definitely pure, but even so, she found it hard to breathe because it was so concentrated, as if every breath that she took sent an infinite number of tiny microscopic pollen particles that hung heavy in the jungle air day and night, into her lungs as they searched for a place to create new life form.

It was another world!

Leaning on the banister, that was beautifully carved out of wood, she wondered how it was possible that in such a short space of time, less than one year, she had come from an old Iraqi neighbourhood, destroyed by bombs, to the Syrian desert, to a smart American University campus, to the solitude of New Mexico and trout-filled idyllic rivers, to the Pacific Ocean and the edgy city of Los Angeles, to the Amazon jungle.

She had gone from being the simple daughter of a middle

class Iraqi family, to being an orphan, a terrorist recruit, a fugitive from justice, to almost being adopted by an eccentric Californian millionaire.

It was all too crazy!

What on earth did this strange woman, who seemed to be hiding such a sinister past, want with her in the first place and why was she clinging to her as if she were the last bit of wreckage to be found on a stormy sea?

Why did she show her so much affection, if she did not harbour the slightest bit of physical attraction for her?

There had been a time when Salka had been on her guard, expecting at any moment that a small gesture or a barely imperceptible reference or an indiscreet look would reveal Mary Lacombe's real intentions to be amorous, but it was not long before the girl realized that her patron was not in the slightest bit interested in her body.

Every night she went to bed asking herself the same question: why had she been chosen like some kind of a rare object? Every morning she woke up with the same question still hanging in the air.

Neither had she found the answer to why a missile had fallen on her house when it had could so easily have fallen elsewhere.

Life! Her life seemed to be marked by a series of inexplicable events, as if she were the victim of the pernicious pranks of a malevolent gang of pixies.

Sometimes she imagined herself to be like the leaf she kept in the pages of her favorite book. A leaf that had fallen from a tree but had managed to defy the laws of gravity because it was formed like a boat and instead of floating down to join the earth's carpet, alongside all the other leaves, it had remained in the air, trapped by a capricious breeze that blew it from side to side. A leaf that danced this way and that without any clear destination, until caught in the slipstream of a car, it changed direction and joined another current of air that whisked it along and straight in to the room of an orphan child, who upon seeing it imagined it to be a message, heaven-sent from her mother and who would keep it forever in the pages of a book and talk to from time to time about her sorrows and loneliness.

It was only a dry leaf, similar to thousands of other dry leaves, except for a barely imperceptible curvature that had helped it escape the bonfire, to become a thing of consolation for a very troubled being.

There was something in the curve of Salka Embarek's lips, the depth of her stare, the brightness of her eyes, and the sincerity with which she pronounced every word, that made her so like that dried leaf that never touched the ground and that had ended up becoming a symbol of hope for someone.

Now she found herself unable to sleep, disorientated by the unfamiliar noises and the quiet of the heavily perfumed night, as she drank in the smells that seeped out of the biggest jungle on earth.

The Congo

Marcel Valerie had managed to hire one of the few houses that had air conditioning in Bukavu, which meant that at least he was able to sit in his office looking out of the window over the lake and read his book.

The fabulous body of the blond Dutch girl he had brought with him from Paris had kept him busy to begin with, but it was not long before he started to feel the suffocating weight of an intense boredom bear down on him and he found himself irritated by the girl, who had started to pace up and down the house like a tortured soul. It was with some relief then, when he came across the extensive and varied work of George Simenon, which served to distract him and ensure that he did not abandon one of the best business opportunities of his life.

He would never know what had attracted the previous owner of the house so fiercely to the writings of his compatriot, but the library there had almost two hundred books by the same author in it, lined up neatly on its shelves, ordered by date of publication.

Marcel Valerie particularly liked the mysterious cases of superintendent Maigret, and if he were honest, the books were better company than the stupid Dutch girl, who kept trying to start up insignificant conversations that would all too quickly descend into unintelligible ramblings.

The mine, the deposit or the factory, or whatever you liked to call it, was being run by an efficient and capable local who had managed to keep things ticking along steadily by notably increasing the salaries of the exploited workers.

It was on one of those insufferably hot mornings that Victor Dacosta paid him a visit. The man from Cape Verde, who was missing an ear, ripped off, he claimed, when a lion attacked him, although rumour had it that it had been cut it off with a knife during an unpleasant exchange at a brothel, walked in without explanation and offered to sell him his deposit.

"Why the sudden decision?" the Belgian said, feigning surprise.

"I'm fed up with this job. The climate in this country is enough to drive anyone to distraction and besides, I miss the sea."

"But you've got the lake."

"A lake is a lake, but I am desperate to go back to Cape Verde."

"Don't lie to me Victor, don't lie," the Belgian said softly, trying to smile affectionately. "This is no way to start up a business conversation. What you really want to do is sell the deposit because the price of coltan is still too low, and you're scared that before long the deposit won't be worth a cent…"

"That's no way to start up a business conversation either," the other man protested.

"You might be right, but at least it's sincere. I would advise you not to be in such a hurry to sell. The crisis may pass and I would prefer you to hang on in there."

"But you need capital to hang on in there in these tough times, and unfortunately I don't have that," the Portuguese man confessed frankly. "My people won't work for me if I don't pay them. The soldiers that protect me won't do so if they don't get their monthly salary, and the officials that authorize my export permits won't sign them unless they receive their commission on time. With prices the way they are, I can hardly cover my costs."

"They'll go up again!"

"Who can guarantee that?"

"Market logic."

"Business dealings in coltan have never been logical Marcel, you know that. It's always been totally unpredictable, from being worth nothing to selling for the same price as gold to falling flat on its face again. It's time for me to cut my losses and run."

"If I were you, then, I'd stop production, lay off the workers and keep the deposit dormant and see what happens in the future."

"For how long?"

"I don't know. A year, maybe two."

Dacosta shook his head, as if he had already decided.

"I can't go back home with one hand in front of me and the other one tied behind, saying that I plan to go back to work in a year or two. I'd prefer to sell out and forget about the Congo forever. What's your final offer?"

Marcel Valerie stood up and walked up and down the large room, all the while looking at the visitor and shaking his head as if unable to believe that he was selling out. He then turned to look out of the window and for a short while appeared to be distracted by a group of people in a canoe, fishing five hundred meters or so off the coast, until finally he replied:

"I don't want to take advantage of the situation Victor, it's not my style. I know only too well what it means to go through bad times and that the hyenas are always lying in wait for the weakest prey. Reconsider it."

"I've spent too much time going over it and I've had enough. You know my deposit well enough, it's almost on the edge of yours. Give me a figure."

Marcel Valerie went over to the table, took out a small calculator from a drawer, tapped in some numbers, studied the result, looked at the ceiling and then turned to look at him directly.

"I can't pay you in cash, but I can give you one million a year for five years."

"With a bank guarantee?"

"Of course."

"Give me that for six and the deposit's yours!"

"Five and a half if you get rid of the workers first. I'm not planning on exploiting the mine until I've properly assessed the market and decided on how important these deposits in the Amazon bowl really are."

Texas

The meeting had been scheduled for eleven o'clock, but just before nine-thirty that same morning, a bullet fired from a telescopic rifle flew through the electric fence that enclosed the guests by way of protection, sliced its way through a white, wide-brimmed hat and lodged itself in Ed Pierce's brain, just as he was stepping out of his luxurious apartment.

It took his wife almost ten minutes for her to realize that she had become a widow.

The bullet had shot through the air so silently and the poor man had been killed so suddenly, that not even the dogs, those stupid dogs, had noticed that the Dall&Houston board of directors now had one less member on its team.

Where had it been fired from?

How many Blackwaters were on guard at the time, and why did it take them so long to realize that something seriously bad had happened?

But more to the point: What on earth were they all doing locked up inside this fortress, when the enemy was actually within their midst?

Jeff Hamilton sat down heavily into his chair and held his head in his hands, totally speechless and seemingly beside himself with the realization that despite all the money he had spent and the precautions he had taken to ensure everyone's safety, he had failed them. His efforts had failed, collapsed in one go, like dominoes in a line, by the actions of one sniper alone.

When Tony Walker put his hand on Jeff Hamilton's shoulder by way of condolence, he lifted his face and said quietly:

"You were right. Mercenaries are mercenaries and when you hire them you can't blame them for betraying you; just as the snake charmer can't complain when he too is poisoned. Cretin! How could I have been such a cretin to have actually believed them?"

"What's done is done. There's no point getting upset over that now," his colleague pointed out. "The point is, what are you going to about it?"

"Offer another two million, impunity and anonymity to whoever did it."

"What's that?" his subordinate asked, hoping that he had misheard. "Did you say, offer him money, impunity and anonymity? Have you gone mad?"

"Not at all! Ed Pierce is dead and nothing will bring him back. At this very moment we have about fifty motherfuckers on the ranch, most of whom are professional assassins and all of whom are now under suspicion of having fired that fatal shot. I doubt we'll find out who actually did it and least of all who paid them to do it. But if we offer to let him walk away freely with double pay, it's quite possible that he'll give us a name. It's as clear as day that the only language they speak is one of money and betrayal. If you've done it once, why wouldn't you do it again?"

"As an argument you have a point…" Tony Walker conceded. "I'm not sure it would work though."

"What is there to lose?"

"Close to a hundred million…" he said quickly, a flicker of humour in his voice. "I think these motherfuckers might well admit to committing a crime they didn't do, just to get their hands on another two million dollars."

"We'll get them to prove that they're guilty."

"Oh come on Peter!" the other guy exclaimed. "What you're proposing is almost Kafkaesque. Ask an assassin who has killed someone in cold blood to prove it and then walk free! What kind of a crazy person would do that?"

"Somebody whose name was on a list of fifteen people sentenced to death, six of whom have already been killed."

"God damn it! That's also a valid argument and I admit that I'd hate to be in your shoes right now, however soft the leather."

"Cut the bullshit, Tony! It's not appropriate."

"I know, I'm sorry, but I really think you're best off leaving this up to Mariel. He was the one that predicted all this after all."

"I don't trust him; apart from the fact that three hundred million is a lot of millions."

"Offer him one hundred for now and the rest when you see some results. If he's that sure of success, as he appears to be, then he'll take you up and if you don't pay him you'll be the first on his list. He never fails."

"I need to think about it."

"Well think smart then, because there's a guy wandering around with a telescopic rifle who may have been asked to double his quota."

Amazon

"It seems totally ridiculous that here I am, by the light of a fire, in the middle of the night, surrounded by exotic animals baying from deep within the jungle, on the shores of a river, infested with alligators, about to justify who I am and what I've done," the old lady began.

"It is equally ridiculous to carry on lying when there is no one around to hear us and I'm entering the last leg of my journey in this world.

"Why should I carry on denying at this stage in life, that I've committed possibly every crime under the sun? Every single crime! I have never felt the need to repent because deep down my soul I didn't actually feel that it had done anything wrong.

"I once sent an entire army to its death, but I felt no need to justify my actions to anybody, least of all to myself. I just did what I had to do as long as it was of some benefit to me, which is all the majority of human beings ever do anyway, including the hypocrites amongst us.

"You, however, living with the memory of your own family, would find it inconceivable that there was someone out there who did not even care about his own mother, but that is the way it was and I don't think it was my fault. I have never loved or hated, and this has been without doubt my greatest punishment. I've heard it said that our passions are the things that make us unique and separate from most of the animal kingdom. Without passion you're like a stone. Most of my life I have been that rock, battered by the waves and winds; the rock that never moves, that never becomes dislodged or loses even a tiny fragment of itself."

They had travelled over the jungle in a helicopter, following the Madeira River right up to its famous waterfalls and they had watched from the air as fires devoured some of the planet's last remaining virgin territory. They had fished for pirarucus weighing about one hundred kilos, in lost tributaries where civilization had never set foot before. They had visited indigenous tribes whose parents had devoured each other, and they had marvelled at the flocks of red ibis, parrots and macaws that flew majestically over the tops of the trees, some forty meters high.

They had bathed in still lakes inhabited by anacondas and they had watched a jaguar hunting for prey on the opposite side of the river.

They had asked hundreds of questions about the fabulous world that surrounded them and they had listened attentively to the answers given to them from people who understood the secrets of the jungle and all its inhabitants.

As the old lady sat underneath the starry sky she continued:

"You can't expect me to bow down and try to justify the unjustifiable; it's not my style. I am what I am and there is nothing or no one to blame for the monstrous crimes I committed, that I was quite aware of committing at the time. The only thing that mattered to me was me, and as soon as I realized that I might be in danger I had no qualms about faking my own death, even if it meant making my own mother suffer that grief.

"Years later, knowing that once again I was being hunted down, I did something that only I was capable of doing: I renounced myself, the man I'd been for half a century and I became a woman. There's no reason to be horrified; nor even be surprised, since I did not care whether I was one sex or the other. I was as indifferent as I'd always been to anything. A complex operation and I don't know how many hormone replacements; a change of wardrobe and that was it, because deep down nothing had changed in me. I was proud of being like that; proud that there had never been nor ever would be anyone like me, and there was nothing I liked more than the constant reaffirmation that I was different from everybody else, totally different from other mortals!

"My story is a bitter one, miserable and totally despicable, as foul as one a snake might recount, had he the gift of speech. But when all is said and done it is my own story."

The eyes of the alligators that sat on the river's surface reflected the fire like flaming coals and when one of them came in too close, the old lady would take out her gun and blow out its eyes with one shot and the animal would sink like a stone and the water would ripple with the movement of its companions, as they moved in to devour the body.

"If one day you manage to accept all this, then everything I've managed to get is yours," she continued. "And it's a lot because I committed many crimes to get it, simply for the pleasure of seeing how I could deceive a society that I simply did not care for.

"Winning for the sake of winning is like a taking a drug that you have to keep on upping the dosage for. The same thing that pushes men to risk their lives by climbing mountains that get higher every time, to drive cars faster or dive deeper every time, pushed me to dream up ever more complicated robberies or complex assassinations. The only tangible difference between me and a serial killer was the fact that while the serial killer only committed murder, my own misdeeds spanned the entire criminal spectrum. So you have to decide on whether or not you are able accept this blood-stained money, or give it up, as I fear you will, which means it will remain in the bank's hands forever. I know that you'll take more pleasure in squandering it than I did in obtaining it, because I never really cared too much for it. Money is capable of destroying a heart, but if there isn't one to begin with then it has little impact."

"But why me?"

"That's another long story and dawn is breaking."

Texas

News that a sixth person had been assassinated inside the ranch that was supposedly under the protection of the Blackwaters security team prompted what nobody would ever have believed possible and that not even the ups and downs of an unjust war had managed to do until now: the Dall&Houston share prices lost eleven per cent of their value on the stock exchange in only four hours and would have continued in their vertiginous descent had their stock not been momentarily suspended. The reason behind the fall was that three of the survivors of what was starting to look like a massacre, had publicly declared the sale of their shares at any price in a desperate attempt to free themselves of any links they had with the company.

They were, it seemed, trying to convince the mysterious terrorist called "Aarohum al Rashid" that it would not make any sense to kill them since, as they had stated to the press: *"The decision to fake the presence of weapons of mass destruction with the aim of invading Iraq had been taken by the main board of directors, which none of them, as simple shareholders, were in a position to effectively oppose."*

The board of directors at that time had been made up of Peter Corkenham and two other members, who were now dead, and controlled from behind the scenes by an all-powerful vice-president.

Whether or not any of this was true, that one man alone had been responsible for this horrific crime, remained to be seen. What was certain nonetheless, was that the seemingly indestructible structure of Dall&Houston had started to weaken.

The owner of Seven Oaks, it was said, would not show his face publicly.

Blackwater's managing director for the West Coast had turned up on the ranch the same day that Ed Pierce was killed, accompanied by twenty of his men that he considered to be incorruptible and who immediately took over the so-called perimeter of maximum security and got on with the thankless task of interrogating every single one of their armed companions in a concerted effort to find out who had betrayed them all in such an ignominious way.

They were upset that the organization's reputation had been sullied and they refused outright to accept the proposal that the guilty party take some money or immunity in exchange for their collaboration.

"Nobody is leaving here with two million dollars in their pocket, at least walking, that is," they muttered convincingly. "We cannot allow this incident to cast doubt over our integrity and for people to think that by hiring us they may well be hiring their very own hangman."

They already had a reputation for using excessive force and violence, for being trigger happy and for having killed, without apparent motives, dozens of innocent civilians in the war-torn city of Baghdad.

But it was one thing to shoot indiscriminately around the streets of a chaotic city at war, without worrying who they hit, and another to kill the shareholder of a company that had given them all lucrative contracts, in cold blood. But where was the rifle that had fired the shot and where had the shot come from?

Officers of the law brought in from Houston and San Antonio carried out all kinds of scientific tests, which revealed that whoever had been capable of firing the bullet that had sliced a white hat in half, from a small window in one the horse stables some six hundred meters away, they had to have been an excellent sniper.

Every one of the five snipers, however, that were considered top of their game and that made up the Blackwater team at Seven Oaks that day, had a watertight alibi.

Maybe it was one of the workers on the ranch? A waiter, a

gardener, a cowboy or caretaker of the golf course?

Logic indicated that on that fateful morning it was most likely to have been one of the fifty or so heavily armed professional killers that had been milling around the place, but in the circumstances, further conjecture had become quite pointless.

The whole situation had become quite Dantesque, almost like a tragic comedy, with hysterical women and crying children all over the place and terrified men staring suspiciously at anyone who approached them. The police and forensic teams meanwhile busied themselves with taking photos and measuring distances, observed from the sidelines by a bunch of sour-faced gunmen in dark shades, with heavy machine guns slung over their chests, who watched their every move.

The interrogators remained there throughout the day and well into the night, speaking to everyone except the horses, who, had they been able to speak, would have pointed directly to the assassin.

The atmosphere had become so strained that the following morning Judy Slater sent an email to Mariel telling him that he could not bear it any longer, informing him of everything that had happened and begging him to save him.

"Our numbers are falling by the day..." he concluded. "So with every day the likelihood that I'll be next increases. Please help me!"

The following afternoon four private detectives, authorized to carry weapons and contracted anonymously by Lee Kitanen, who as usual was taking orders from Mariel, turned up at Seven Oaks in two blacked out vehicles, with strict orders to take Judy Slander and his family to another place that was "really safe".

That was a big blow to the reputation of the feared Blackwaters.

The Dall&Houston shares prices continued to plummet.

Congo

The beautiful Dutch woman certainly had a fantastic body and was very obliging in bed. As soon as she lay down she would just open up her legs, and remain that way, in a trance-like state, as Marcel Valerie positioned his head in between them and slid his tongue inside her, in one long, intense movement. His efforts were more often than not, rewarded with a soft but firm snort, but rarely anything more exciting than that.

He would often remain in that position for hours and end up with a neck ache that sometimes threatened to become chronic. Still, trying to achieve the impossible was one way of passing the torrid Congolese afternoons, his only other option being to get his head stuck into another George Simenon novel.

Anyhow, the smell that came from between the Dutch girl's legs was much more appetizing than the smell that emanated from those old, musty and dog-eared books.

Marcel Valerie was in this customary position, although this time half asleep on the smooth muscles from which so much pleasure could be derived, had they, on this occasion been able to do so by themselves, when the maid knocked inconsiderately at their door to tell him brusquely that "a white man" was there to see him.

The white man that awaited him was no ordinary man, but none other than the very persistent and much feared Alex Fosset, who, it was said, had taken part in as many wars as he had lived years, and was also rumored to have actually started a few of them himself.

To look at, however, he was so thin he verged on the scrawny, the little hair he had was thinning, and his two beady eyes stared out from behind a pair of small glasses without frames. He looked more like a village priest or one of those shady council workers whose name no one ever remembered.

It was hard to accept that this man, this pathetic example of a human being, with a high-pitched voice and unashamedly camp mannerisms, was responsible for the deaths of over one thousand people.

His only saving grace was his ability to get straight to the point.

"You need protection," was the first thing he said. "*My* protection, because it won't be long before the gangs of bandits and rebels that run wild in this border zone start to attack your mines and factories."

"I was afraid of that," the Belgian replied curtly, having already heard the pitiful tale of the continent's most hideous and bloody mercenary, before he had moved to Bukavu. "They warned me that sooner or later you'd be paying me a visit."

"Well here I am!" the slimy man said cockily. "What are you planning to do about it?"

Marcel Valerie opened up the safe, took out an envelope and handed it to his disagreeable and impromptu guest.

"It's what they gave me for you, and before you complain take a look at the numeration on the note."

Alex Fosset opened the packet slowly, took out a one hundred dollar note and studied the numeration on it carefully, then, looking thoroughly pleased with the payment, he stood up.

"Agreed!" he said. "From now on all my men will be at your service. Nobody will dare come anywhere near you, your factories or mines. Good afternoon!"

Amazon

"Over many years my organization gained a reputation for being the most efficient, impenetrable, and the safest entity in the entire country, capable of carrying out any type of work, ranging from the assassination of a foreign leader in some far flung corner of the world, to bank robberies to faking an accident that left no trace. Top professionals like to finish a job off cleanly and be able to move on without hindrance, but above all they like to be able to count on total impunity…" she smiled vaguely, threw another log on the fire and said after a brief pause, "I would be lying if I said I hadn't enjoyed what I did. When I was very young I read a strange book called *The Fine Arts of the Assassin*, and all of my actions were centred around exactly that.

"I catalogued them all in the same way that a work of art is catalogued. I know it's hard for you to understand that, but try and put yourself in the shoes of somebody that doesn't have any family, friends, loves, or vices. I would spend hours dreaming up dark plots, with an unnatural desire to put my imagination to the test, like one of those computer games where you are continually being challenged to speed up your reflexes and push up your score."

"Except that you were actually killing in real life."

"You said it! My dead men actually died, I won't deny that, and other than on the one occasion when one of my men made a stupid mistake and two children drowned, I never regretted a thing. Most of those that I sent over to the other side did not deserve to continue living on this one; which is not a justification, just a fact. I never justify myself, as it would be like admitting that I was guilty of things and I've never felt that emotion."

"But that guilt exists," Salka persisted.

"I am also aware that love, hate, friendship, rage, revenge, resentment, jealousy, fear, desire, anxiety and desperation all exist, but I have never felt any of them," the old lady countered.

"I feel sorry for you."

"What a stupid thing to say little girl...! You have suffered a thousand times more in your short life than I have, despite the fact I am nearly three times your age."

"Nothing can compare with the pain that my family disappearing has caused me, but it would have been worse to have never known them and loved them for all those years."

"How do you know that?" the old lady retorted, with a slightly aggressive edge to her voice. "And how do you know that it would have been better for me to have loved and lost? In my opinion this is a subject that smacks of conjecture."

There was a long and thoughtful silence as they contemplated the fire, the river full of alligators lying in wait, until finally and fearing her answer, Salka Embarek asked:

"Why did you want to get to know me then?"

"Because of the one sentiment I have never been able to dominate: curiosity," was the sincere reply. "About a year ago, Dall&Houston who I had worked for many times before, asked me to organize an assassination in the same vein as the one carried out on John F Kennedy. As befitted my meticulous nature, I asked them to find me a scapegoat who would admit to being guilty, just as they did with Lee Harvey Oswald.

"A short time after that, I heard of a girl who had lost her family during one of the first night air raids in Baghdad, and that she had sworn to avenge herself by becoming a suicide bomber, by which I mean you. They told me that you were young, resolute, brave, and intelligent, that you spoke English perfectly and had an unusual character, but that you were terribly naïve and had no idea that you were being used.

"I'd heard so much about you that I decided I had to meet this person who was prepared to blow herself up into tiny fragments in defence of her ideals, a concept that was quite simply inconceivable to someone like me. So curiosity led me that afternoon to you. I arrived in my bright caravan to the place where I knew you would be waiting on that day in your life when you thought you'd been saved, but in fact you were closer to death than ever. I invited you to have supper and you accepted. The following day I invited you to go fishing and you accepted.

"But luckily for you the plot was exposed before its time, the assassination was aborted and there was no need for you to die. The rest you already know."

Salka Embarek fixed her stare on the flames that danced before her eyes as she tried to take in everything that Mary Lacombe had just told her.

It was hard to guess what was going through her head at that moment. Her companion, allowing her some time for reflection, took to raking the fire with a long stick, sending sparks flying into the night and deep in to Amazon jungle.

When the night bird stopped its squawking, a silence descended over the jungle that was so intense you could almost hear the agitated heard beat of the old lady who sat there, patiently awaiting the girl's response.

Finally turning her head only slightly, the young girl looked her in the eyes and asked:

"What would you have done if the plot had not been discovered in time?"

"Nothing."

"You would have let them kill me?"

"Of course."

"You're a wretched son of a bitch with no feelings."

"I always have been," Mary Lacombe admitted quite casually. She paused briefly before continuing, "The only thing that I ask of you is that you don't judge me for what I was but what I am now."

"It's not that easy to simply erase the past when you feel like it."

"But I'm not trying to erase it. I take full responsibility for it and I'm not asking for forgiveness or understanding," came her steadfast reply.

"That is bad; that you can't even repent," she said, shaking her head sadly. "It would be very difficult to understand someone like you. You're a brick wall."

"You're probably right," the old woman agreed. "I've always been a brick wall, even to myself, but the basic issue now and one which I am asking you to consider, is that you have a choice between the woman you now know and the man that I have been telling you about, that you never knew and that maybe never even existed in reality."

"What do you mean by that?"

"That maybe the story of Mauro Rivero and Mariel are pure fantasies."

"But they're not fantasies," the girl retorted.

"No! They are real, but maybe you could get used to the idea that it was all an invention and in that way be at peace with yourself."

"Don't play games with me," the girl muttered under her breath. "I don't like it and it's not your style. I prefer it when you are as brutally honest as you usually are. You are right, it's up to me to choose between the Mary I know and the person I never did. But this is not the time or place for that decision to be made, I would rather do it in Los Angeles. When are we going?"

"Tomorrow."

California

"It's a firm proposal: one hundred million and the rest as soon as the information is verified. If our people accept it, then it'll be up to them to see it through, this will ensure that your organisation avoids any type of confrontation with Al Rashid's men."

"When you talk about our men are you referring to the Blackwaters?" the hooded man with the deep voice, sitting on the other side of the table, asked.

"Not necessarily."

"You'd have to guarantee me that, because I have very little confidence in that bunch of suburban killers. They're useless and would betray their own mothers if pushed. I wouldn't even put them in charge of setting up a tent and under the protection of Bush's laws. They've got used to walking around like a herd of elephants in a china shop, for which reason I am just not prepared to put my organization, which has taken me thirty years to build, at risk."

Tony Walker sighed and it was obvious that he felt uncomfortable, as uncomfortable as he always felt whenever he came face to face with the formidable Mariel, combined with the fact that this time they were discussing an issue that was particularly delicate.

"And who do you think we should recruit if we decide not to use the Blackwaters, who we normally collaborate with?" he asked.

"Maybe the Russian mafia could give us a hand, the Albanians or the Sicilians, but if you want my advice I would go for the Calabrian Ndranghetas. The first of those two are very violent and do not have the subtlety required for this job, while the Sicilians, who are undoubtedly the most well prepared, are in my opinion, in cahoots with the people they claim to be fighting."

"This worries me."

"And me too. Which is why my price is so high and my desire to get involved so low."

"All right! I'll take your advice and try and get hold of the Ndranghetas. What can you tell me about Al Rashid?"

"That he never actually existed; at least not as the justice-seeking avenger in search of money to rebuild his beloved Iraq with."

Tony Walker took some time to digest this news before saying:

"I don't know why, but that news doesn't surprise me."

"I've always thought of you as an intelligent man."

"Thanks for the compliment, but in this case it's not about intelligence, just pure intuition. His request was too romantic somehow and the days of Robin Hood are long gone. Where does all this Islamic terrorist paraphernalia come from then?"

"These days it gets banded around whenever something needs a cover up. My advice is that you try and pick out something cleanly. Concentrate on just one of the assassins and from there you may pick up the scent that will lead to your prey."

"I suppose you're referring to the murder of Vincent Kosinsky. In my opinion that was an excessively sophisticated set up and threw out too many unknowns."

"Very perceptive on your part," Mariel acknowledged with a slight smile. "Kosinsky was a crazy man, a confirmed alcoholic and incredibly rich, with no family and a way of life that was irreverently wild. After his death nobody found a will and nobody seemed at all bothered about where he might have hidden his fabulous fortune, which I found interesting so I subsequently investigated. I found out of course, that the money he had invested in the shares of countless companies, the details of all his coded accounts held in tax free havens, and his famous diamond collection, had all been kept inside an enormous safe box in the Cactus Flower, where he'd lived for the last eighteen years."

"Are you sure of that?"

"Totally sure!" he replied swiftly. "I got hold of old video recordings of inside the casino, which has cameras everywhere, even in the bathrooms. Imagine Gigi Trotta's face every time that irresponsible drunk, who never bothered taking security measures, the state he was usually in, punched in his access code and opened up the safe box revealing all that treasure inside it?"

"It must have been excruciatingly tempting."

"Especially for a member of the mafia whose casino was losing money and urgently needed a complete makeover. I suspect that Gigi Trotta, who carried the keys and knew by heart the combination that he had seen punched in a thousand times before, had something to do with all that. I bet you that when the police went to open Kosinsky's safe box they probably found a bit of loose change and not a trace of all those shares, the diamonds or the coded bank accounts."

"That would be one logical explanation," his listener conceded. "And convincing at that. As far as I know, Kosinsky owned about three percent of the shares in Dall&Houston and was on the board of directors of many other big multinationals, which means he must have been sitting on an absolute fortune. What a peculiarly eccentric character!"

"Eccentric or not, he certainly knew how to enjoy his money. He squandered it without qualms."

"Do you think I should tell all this to the police?"

"That's your decision, not mine," came his curt reply as he started to drum his fingers on the desk once again. "But remember you don't have any proof of what I just said and with so much money at stake, the investigation could go on forever. In this country, thanks to the hysteria generated by the Bush administration, you only have to say the word "terrorist" and anything goes... and is then forgiven."

He got up, signalling that the interview had come to an end.

"My advice is to get some Calabrian guys on to Gigi, who

have historically always been enemies of the Sicilians and don't get the police involved in this at all."

"But how do we get the Dall&Houston shares back?"

"I've not got the faintest idea, my friend. Not the faintest! But if you want me to find out where they went, you'll have to give me ten per cent of what I find."

"I'll check with my bosses."

"You know where to find me of course! As you leave they'll give you a copy of the tapes from the Cactus Flower and you'll be able to see exactly what was in Kosinsky's safe box. That's on the house."

He disappeared behind a heavy door and Tony Walker remained there, stock still, waiting for someone to collect him, blindfold him and return him to his car.

Amazon

A timber barge, heading down the Amazon river from deep within Rondonia, had run aground on a bank of sand and several trunks had fallen off near the shore. Quite peculiarly, some of the bigger ones had partially sunk.

When the authorities investigated this strange phenomenon they discovered that the insides of the trunks that did not float were filled with a strange and unfamiliar mineral.

Word soon got out that coltan was being exported as contraband from deep within the Amazon jungle.

Despite the efforts taken by the traffickers to hide the evidence, this new discovery could not be ignored and only served to confirm that some of the logging teams that claimed to be cutting down forests deep within the jungle, were in fact extracting a valuable mineral.

Word also got out that Victor Dacosta from Cape Verde had closed down a concession that was no longer producing and that a Belgian guy had bought it from him, who believed that coltan would soon be as lucrative as it had once been.

Once the deal had become public knowledge, Marcel Valerie was inundated with requests from other mine owners wanting 'out' and all asking for an agreement similar to the one he had signed with the man from Cape Verde.

"I'm sorry!" he felt obliged to apologize repeatedly. "So sorry, but I don't have as much money as it would appear. If I buy your concession and the price continues to plummet, I'll be ruined."

He still managed, however, to sign agreements with several of the owners of the more lucrative deposits by advancing them small amounts of money and agreeing to offer them a percentage of earnings if things improved in the future.

He also demanded that every agreement be kept secret at all costs, since, as he put it: he did not want "all and sundry" knocking at his door.

He also left the country for a while and headed for Europe, where he hoped to find new investors that would be prepared to take the same risks and who shared in his belief that coltan would once again become a lucrative business option, despite the increasingly poor market conditions.

'Miraculously' he found some investors, and against all odds managed to increase the amount of business associates he had in the Congo quite significantly, who were, by then, virtually eating out of his hands.

The mineworkers, however, were not so happy, as their jobs, awful though they were, disappeared before their very eyes as one deposit after another was closed down.

The gangs of armed men who had been employed to transport the precious metal also found themselves without work, while a certain amount of powerful companies in different parts of the world watched on helplessly as an avalanche of the metal hit the market, pushing prices down and ruining their businesses.

Even the Brazilian government had started to think about pushing up the price of the concessions it was planning to tender for exploitation in Rondonia, if it could only confirm that, as evidence increasingly suggested, the area was home to some important reserves of coltan.

Los Angeles

As soon as she had finished her breakfast and drunk her last cup of tea, Mary Lacombe opened the box that she had next to her, took out an album covered in soft white leather and placed it in front of Salka Embarek.

"What's this?" the girl asked, without touching it.

"Photos."

"Of our trip to Brazil?"

"Not exactly."

"Well...?"

"Wouldn't it be easier to open it up and then ask the questions, my dear?" the old lady said smiling gently. "There are some things that are best to look at, rather than talk about."

Salka felt strangely apprehensive, as if the beautiful object with her initials printed in gold on the front of it, held something inside that might unsettle her.

She looked at her companion, then opened the album very slowly. She stared at the first page, totally mesmerised by the four photos on it as a large tear slipped down her cheek and onto her napkin.

She remained like that for a while, unable to speak as she looked and looked again at the photos, as if unable to believe her own eyes.

Finally she had to ask:

"Why have you done this?"

"Because I know what it means to you. I sent a detective to Baghdad who was able to find photos of you with your parents and brothers and sisters, at children's birthday parties and family gatherings, and that's how we managed to find out what furniture you had, every carpet, every picture, right down to the sets of plates and glasses you used. When you go back to your house, you'll be able to put it back together, just as it was before that abominable missile destroyed it."

"What a waste of time," the Iraqi girl said desperately, overwhelmed with emotion. "I don't know if I'll ever go back to Baghdad."

"You will go back dear! You will return because part of you is still there. One day, this hideous war will end and it will be the *city of a thousand and one nights* once again and you'll be able to enjoy candlelit evenings under the moon in your garden, in your house that will have been rebuilt. Once the storm has passed, the runaway streams return to their original source. The dead don't come back but the landscape remains the same."

"How will I ever be able to thank you?"

"Quite simply by accepting my money that will one day help you to rebuild your house; the college where you studied; the square where you played; the streets that you walked through holding your mother's hand and even the bridge that your brothers used play on."

"You've got that much money?"

"Yes. And I'm planning on getting even more from the people that are guilty of destroying your house, your college, your square, your streets and your bridge."

"Blood money."

"Blood money used to rebuild with is surely better than new money used to destroy with… or is it not?"

"I don't know what to say."

"Yes you do," the old lady said briskly. "When all this is over, when this brainless president steps down and the soldiers go home, when the white-gloved assassins are sent to rot in prison or are buried two meters underground, peace will return to your country. Iraq will need money, even if this money is stained with blood, it was money that was taken from you and your people, and it belongs to you."

"You can be very convincing sometimes."

"Sometimes, but please my dear, don't offend me. It's been my job to convince people and betray them whenever necessary, and I've excelled at that. But I'm not trying to deceive you now; just convince you."

"You swore that you'd would never try and justify the crimes you have committed," Salka Embarek pointed out. "But now I get the feeling that you are doing exactly that."

"You are mistaken, little one. I'm not trying to justify them. I'm trying to do something that gives me some personal satisfaction. I am now journeying through the last chapter of my life. I've got millions in the bank and it doesn't give me the slightest bit of pleasure. But to know that you could rebuild your house with this money and how much that would mean to you, gives me a feeling of satisfaction."

"You are still trying to manipulate me," Salka exclaimed.

"Not at all. Manipulation requires the victim to be totally ignorant of the facts, but in this case you know exactly what my intentions are. The only thing I'm trying to do is seduce you, in the better sense of the word, and hope that despite your stubborn nature, you realize that it would be stupid of you to turn down my offer."

"I do not have a stubborn nature," the increasingly irate Salka Embarek protested. "What's happening is very confusing, which can only be expected if you look at all the absurd things that have happened to me lately. And here I am now embroiled with this strange and inhumane person that calls herself Mary Lacombe."

"Don't get ahead of yourself, little girl. Remember it was me that went looking for you, which makes your present situation no more than the consequence of a series of events that started the day your family was killed" she said sharply.

"If you'd stayed behind in Baghdad, as hundreds of girls in the same circumstances did and who are now wandering the streets, many of them as prostitutes, we would never have met. The first absurd event happened when you made the decision to avenge all that you had lost, rather than resign yourself to it.

Everything that's happened since has done so as a result of your actions alone, and until you accept this, however much it hurts, you will continue to feel confused. Am I making myself clear?"

"You are forever clarifying things."

"I'll dig my heels in on this one. When a young girl takes the decision to blow herself up into tiny pieces in order to take I don't how many people with her, people she considers to be her enemies, but who might well be innocent and may well have been opposed to the war in the first place, you have to accept that from that point on anything might happen. The worst case scenario being that one day your head turns up in the middle of the street and your leg in a gutter, and thanks be to God this has not happened."

"It's like you're thanking God and not yourself."

"Touché! I believe you might have a point, but you must have realized by now that I've always been a complete son of bitch without feelings."

Las Vegas

The bedside lamp was switched on and Gigi Trotta woke up with a start, and not without good reason, as he found himself staring down the barrel of a gun, that was pointed directly between his eyes.

"Good evening Gigi!" someone said in a strong Italian accent, who reeked of alcohol. "Where are the diamonds?"

He lifted himself up, but kept himself flat against the embossed bed head, in an attempt to see the face behind the weapon being brandished in front of him.

He did not recognize him, or the fat man standing next to him.

"What diamonds?" he finally stuttered.

"Come on Gigi!" the intruder said insistently, without altering the tone of his voice. "Don't play the fool. You know perfectly well that I'm referring to Kosinsky's diamonds that he kept in the safe box and that were worth a fortune."

"I don't know what you're talking about."

"Listen imbecile!" the other one said, starting to get annoyed. "We've seen from the video tapes that inside the safe box there were three red velvet bags, that no one has seen since. And we believe they contain the diamonds. Where are they?"

"I promise you I don't know."

"You are lying to me, mascalzone, we know full well that you struck a deal with someone to get rid of the old drunk and then divided up the winnings fifty-fifty, which means that you must have the diamonds. Give them up now or we'll turn this place upside down and wake up the boys asleep at the end of the passage, which would be bad news for them as I'm not fond of leaving witnesses around the place, if you know what I mean. Your two thugs are snoring in bed right now and dreaming the dreams of honest men."

The revolver's barrel was almost scraping his nose now, as the intruder continued, "Don't worry about yourself, you've not got much time left anyway; but think of your innocent boys and how it's not their fault that their father is a dirty trouble maker that betrays his own club members."

"You wouldn't do them any harm...!" the director of the Cactus Flower was on the verge of tears. "They're only children!"

"That depends on you 'filiotto'. We have received very clear orders: we return with three bags of diamonds, or we leave behind a bunch of bodies as a warning that the person in charge of this operation is not playing games."

Gigi Trotta was dripping with sweat, his hands trembled and he found it hard to speak, harder still to think, so with the tip of his finger he very gently pushed the revolver a few centimetres away from him.

"I hid them in the casino's safe box."

"There's nothing valuable in the safe box, caro mío. We just checked it. Three thousand and something dollars, four or five insurance policies, some divorce papers and an old pocket watch that his grandfather probably brought him from Palermo. But, not a diamond to speak of. Where have you hidden them?"

Gigi Trotta, trembling with fear in the face of his defeat, his sheets now soaked with urine, made a limp gesture towards a large lamp with an imitation Roman amphora base on it, standing on a table on the other side of the room. The fat guy went over to it, lifted it up, examined it carefully, unscrewed the base of it and took out three red velvet bags.

He went back over to them and emptied their contents on to the bed.

"My God!"

"How much is this worth?" the man pointing the gun at Gigi Trotta asked. "Have you any idea?" Gigi Trotta shook his head as the other one added contemptuously, "What a shame! It seems a pity to die without knowing how much your life was worth."

"We could share it out and nobody would know any better," Gigi tried.

"Somebody would find out, bambino, and I'd be the one woken up in the middle of the night by a pair of bastards, one of them holding a gun to my head. That's what makes people piss in their beds as far as I can make out and I did enough of that as a child."

He stretched out his hand, grabbed a pillow, put it over his victim's face, pushed the gun into it and fired a single shot.

Gigi Trotta's brain exploded all over the wall behind him.

The two men started putting the diamonds back into their bags, apparently in no hurry to leave, as the fat one picked up a pink stone, the size of a chickpea and turned it over admiringly in his fingers, before turning to his companion with a conspiratorial look.

The other guy shrugged his shoulders and looking over to the blood-soaked pillow said:

"Forget it! You know who we're up against."

With a deep sigh of resignation the fat man placed the beautiful stone back in to the bag and left the room, not, however, before turning off the light and shutting the door.

Los Angeles

Salka Embarek still found it impossible to understand how such a fragile old lady, with such a gentle voice, amiable smile and innocent face and who was finding it harder to walk by the day without dragging her feet and whose face had started to reflect the terrible pain she was in, could have been that out and out son of a bitch devoid of all feelings, and the brain behind the most notorious and well respected criminal organization in the country.

Her answer had an element of humour in it:

"It's like trying to imagine how Liz Taylor could ever have been the ethereal and fascinating character in *Cat on a Hot Tin Roof* after more recent photos of her in the papers that showed her looking over one hundred kilos and in a wheelchair. But I was neither old, sweet, friendly nor innocent. I was a "mother fucker" with a moustache and more stings than a squid, capable of imitating thirty different voices in four different languages and fucking over who ever I felt like, without blinking an eyelid.

"Would I be mistaken into thinking that the Salka who strapped explosives to her body and planned to blow herself up was the same girl that used to go for walks with her mother on the banks of the Euphrates?"

"She was not the same girl, no..." the girl admitted. "But my story was circumstantial and I hope that I have put most of it behind me now, whereas I suspect you are still involved in one way or another," she added perceptively.

"I had decided to stop working since I wasn't getting any satisfaction out of it any more, but circumstances have changed and I've changed my mind."

"What circumstances?"

"A challenge has come up."

"A challenge?" the girl repeated.

"Exactly. For a time I collaborated with Dall&Houston, while they were really screwing a whole load of people over, and I feel the time has now come to screw them over."

"You talk about it like you're doing it on a whim, which doesn't really feel like a substantial enough answer."

"It would be even less valid if I said that it was a question of conscience. Imagine that you're always playing roulette and betting on the red so that every time the ball spun, you tried hard for your color to come up. And you win! But then you change your mind and go for the black and you try just as hard to get the black. And you win! You soon realize that you're able to win no matter which way you stack your chips. That's how it is for me. And if after everything I've told you, you haven't understood that the only thing I've done in my life is set and accept challenges, then you still don't know me. And this one, I swear, will be the biggest challenge yet."

"And am I allowed to know what that is?"

The old lady agreed with a slight nod of the head.

"Maybe it's time I cleared a few things up..." she began.

"The Dall&Houston"directors have offered me a lot of money to find out who the real Al Rashid is, that is to say who is killing its board members, challenging me with something that no one else has managed to achieve so far, whilst, they believe, feeding my ego. But for a while now I've felt like they've underestimated my powers of intelligence, which is annoying me and this audacity could well cost them dearly, because it may be the case, and I stress "maybe" that someone on the Dall&Houston board of directors themselves is behind this whole nasty affair."

"To what end?"

"That's what I need to find out and I have to go through the organization to carry out that enquiry."

"I would like to know how it works."

"I thought you'd never ask..."

That same afternoon, just as it started to get dark, they left the house on the cliff and headed south in one of Mary Lacombe's cars, along the coastal road that ran alongside Malibu beach and straight in to the heart of the city of Santa Monica, where they parked the car in a parking lot belonging to a block of flats that was situated just a few minutes walk away from the Mac Arthur park.

"This building belongs to one of my companies," the old lady pointed out by way of explanation, as she opened up the remote-controlled metal doors and they drove into a spacious garage, two floors underground. Only once they were inside and the metal door had closed firmly behind them did they get out of the car. She pressed a button and the wall at the end of the garage opened to reveal another identical garage, with only one car in it.

From the second parking lot they took a private lift up to an apartment on the top floor.

"Et voila!" the old lady exclaimed with a sweeping gesture that took in dozens of computers, telephones and huge screens, all on desks with rotating chairs in front of them. "This is where I manage the Corporation from."

"Incredible!"

"Can't anyone trace you and all this Nasa-like equipment?"

"Nobody, because although the building is mine, I rent it out to several companies. There are so many computers and telephone lines in it that it would take somebody months of research to work out which entrance cable belonged to which floor or which office. If an intruder tried to access the control boxes, my mobile would send me a message to warn me," she said and with a slight smile added, "As soon as I was notified all I'd have to is punch in a few numbers and the whole get up would burn down in minutes."

"Have you always been so forward thinking?"

"In this line of work you don't get to my age having escaped prison unless you've been incredibly forward thinking."

"Teach me how it all works," Salka said again.

"The most important thing is that you memorize and remember all of the access codes for every computer and every mobile telephone, in order to avoid falling into the traps that I've created and to ensure that nobody gets hold of my information, because I never write anything down."

The old lady turned on one screen after another as she spoke.

"In the unlikely event that a hacker was clever enough, and many of them are, to download the material from one of these computers, it would only contain a fraction of the whole piece of information. Every time I send a message I cut it up into twelve pieces and send each one to one of the nearly three billion different email addresses out there, which means that if you don't know which address they've been sent to, then you've got to look through nearly three billion of them. The famous Enigma machine that the Nazis used in the last war had a capacity of only one hundred thousand characters per letter, which meant that a message with one hundred letters on it had a one in ten million chance of being decoded, which they thought was practicably unbreakable. My system is about three billion times more difficult to violate."

"These figures are making me dizzy."

"I've enjoyed putting together and structuring this whole system. If for any reason one of these computers was violated, an acid substance would erase the memory of all the other computers, so destroying all the other bits of information."

"Wouldn't it matter if you lost all that work."

"I'd never lose it my dear. I have external memory deposits that I keep in safes in various banks so that I could sort it all out in under a month. But if they got to me there, then there would be no way of recovering it all."

"How on earth did you develop such sophisticated and complex systems?"

"With a lot of practice and a lot of patience, and in the knowledge that I was up against the FBI, the CIA, the Treasury department, the Tax office, the Pentagon and the secret services in most countries. The advantage I have over them being that they've got too much on their plates to worry about; their members have wives, children, lovers and vices to attend to, whilst I've only ever had to worry about one thing: myself."

"And has all that effort been worth it?" the Iraqi girl asked.

"One hundred per cent darling. I have a cosmetics factory, a film production company, a chain of large stores, twelve office buildings, thousands of shares in some of the best blue chip companies around, a private plane, the best mansion on the coast, fourteen cars and current accounts in thousands of banks. The most important element of which, is that whilst I was building all this, I managed to keep myself entertained," she said, surveying proudly the overwhelming amount of apparatus that surrounded them.

"If it weren't for the hundreds of hours I have spent here, dreaming up all manner of protection systems, crimes and dirty tricks, my life would have turned into a wasteland without reason a long time ago..." she looked at her watch and then smiling maliciously she said, "I think the time has come to make a call to Sicily."

Sicily

Nino Trotta was sleeping soundly in his house in Palermo when the phone rang and an unknown caller, who spoke an almost perfect Italian, told him that whoever had blown the head off his son, whose bloody body had been discovered by his innocent nephews, was affiliated to the Californian branch of the reviled Calabrian Ndrangheta group.

"The Aicardi...?" he said, almost eating his words.

"You said it, not me."

"What else can you tell me?"

"That they took three bags of diamonds from your son and a load of shares in Dall&Houston, a powerful North American company."

"I know the company."

"In that case look for someone interested in owning those shares. They will be the true instigators of Gigi's death, and whoever did that also has the diamonds."

"Why are you telling me all this?"

"Because the enemies of my enemies are my friends."

They hung up and Nino Trotta lay awake for the rest of the night.

With the first light of day he went straight to his youngest son Salvatore's house and woke him up.

"Get dressed! You're leaving on a plane for Rome in a few hours where you'll pick up another plane to Los Angeles. Your cousin Benito will be waiting for you at the airport."

"What am I doing in Los Angeles?"

"Avenging the death of your brother."

Salvatore Trotta never argued with family orders, least of all from the patriarch, and he realized that this was no time to start doing so either, so he packed up his things and drove in haste to the airport, whilst listening to his instructions and what he had to do from the moment he landed in California.

His cousin Benito was waiting for him at the airport with a clear set of plans.

"There are at least twenty Aicardi ice-cream shops in this state and several others in Nevada and Texas, but the real business that these pigs run is prostitution, male and female, which doesn't, of course, stop them from taking on other important jobs from time to time."

"Right."

"They behave as if they're respectable business men and the patriarch, who is almost certainly called Salvatore, can normally be found in the biggest and smartest of their shops on Rodeo Drive Avenue. The place is famous for its clientele that often includes film stars but mainly serves the city's young and aspiring actors who go there, hoping to be discovered. I hate to say it but beneath this elegant façade, the ice cream shop is just a rat's nest where even the waiters are carrying *Berettas* under their aprons.

"How are we going to get in?"

"By using the old 'unblocking the pipes' ruse. You'll be able to watch it all from the Presidential Palace, where you have a reservation."

He actually had a suite on the top floor of the Beverly Hills Wilshire Hotel that sat at one end of Rodeo Drive Avenue and it was there, from his room's large terrace, that Salvatore Trotta was able sit back and watch the day's events unfold before him.

It was just before midday when a yellow van drove slowly down the street, where some of the city's smartest boutiques could be found, and almost simultaneously the whole street started to stink badly of gas.

Some of the pedestrians started to look a little worried, while the shop assistants came out on to the street to see if they could find out where the awful smell was coming from. It came as no surprise when a few minutes later two red cars appeared, blocking off the traffic on both ends of the avenue and a dozen fire men jumped off a large tanker and started to run from one side of the street to another shouting orders, taking air samples and unravelling hoses.

Some minutes later in response to a loud whistle, six high pressure water hoses were turned on and water went crashing through the famous shop windows and doors of the Aicardi ice-cream shop, destroying everything in its path, sending tables and chairs, counters and shelves flying, bringing the clients, employees and three bodyguards who did not have time to get their guns out, to the floor, all of which created such a noisy disturbance that Salvatore Trotta could hear absolutely everything from where he was sitting.

With the water gushing out of six hose pipes and splashing furiously against the ceilings and walls of the shop, everything, including the cash register and a stunned Salvatore Aicardi, who was flaying about as if he had been ship-wrecked in the middle of a huge ocean, was swept out on to the street.

It was as if a giant aquarium had exploded in the heart of the chicest artery in California, the only difference being that instead of brightly coloured fish spilling out on to the pavement you saw bloody, mangled, half-drowned and terrified human beings falling out onto it.

The bewildered patriarch of the main branch of the Calabrian mafia on the West Coast did not even have time take stock of what had really happened, because as soon as he started to come round, some "firemen" lifted him up by the armpits and put him into one of the red cars that had driven up to the scene of disaster.

Five minutes later and only once they were out of sight, the "firemen" got rid of their heavy uniforms, having already abandoned their tanker opposite what had once been the most exclusive ice-cream shop in the whole of Los Angeles.

From his privileged viewpoint, Salvatore Trotta could only

smile as he thought to himself that his cousin Benito might have taken the "unblocking of the pipes" scenario a step too far.

California

"Ex-commander of North American troops in Iraq, the retired General Richard Sánchez, has issued an unusually harsh critique of the Iraq war, which, he maintains has turned in to a "never ending nightmare" the direct result of the "incompetent" Bush Administration that has tried but failed to manage the conflict.

"Sánchez, who was in command in Iraq for a period of one year, has said that he is pessimistic regarding the Government's plans for Iraq, which he sees as a series of "desperate' attempts to achieve stability in a situation where this is no longer a realistic option." "After more than four years of combat, the United States continues with its desperate struggle in Iraq without a single effective strategy in place that could lead to victory, the same applies to the bigger conflict outside the country and its incompetent war against extremism", he stated.

"Although there have been other generals and officials that have criticised the war previously, Richard Sánchez is the most veteran of any of the military men to have expressed such a staunch critique of the way this conflict has been managed.

"Sánchez was never accused of being in any way responsible for torture, but was obliged to abandon his post after that episode and he was never given any further responsibilities until he was forced to retire in 2006.

"Speaking to journalists, Sánchez said: "Our leaders continue to believe that victory can only be achieved by military force, but these military strategies are manipulative and incoherent, making it impossible for victory of any kind to be achieved."

"During his time in Iraq, General Sánchez was among those that ratified, albeit by his silence, the strategy that totally underestimated the capabilities of the insurgents and believed that the deployment of a reduced number of troops would be sufficient to control the situation in Iraq. When General Casey was put in charge, the war's direction changed and he concentrated the troops on combat and insurgency. It

then became obvious that the estimates for the number of troops required in Iraq had been incorrect and that the post-war design attributed to the then Secretary of Defence Donald Rumsfeld and the Vice-president Dick Cheney, had been wrong."

Mary Lacombe put the clipping to one side and turned to face Salka Embarek, who was absorbed in another daily newspaper.

"It was definitely high time that somebody spoke out on this subject," she commented.

"What are you referring to?"

"To General Sánchez's remarks about Iraq."

"I read them too...," Salka said. "It wasn't bad what the ex-President Carter said about Vice-President Cheney either: 'He is a military man that skipped military service, but later emerged as one the greatest advocates of the theory that force is the most efficient method of getting what you want out of this world. This has been a disaster for the country and the reason why the Bush government will go down in history as the worst one ever.'"

"He's absolutely right. Only too often it's the cowards who skip military service that end up more determined than anyone else to put other peoples' lives at risk."

"The question we have to ask ourselves is, what did Saddam Hussein do, by ruling Iraq in a way he felt was appropriate, that is in fact so different from what the Americans have done there since."

"The difference is that nobody will judge them or hang them by the neck, unless the Iraqis decide to invade the United States, which is highly improbable."

"Do you mean to say that they will never be judged?"

"The big difference between the crimes of a dictator and those of a democracy is that the latter tends to enjoy a degree of impunity, my dear girl."

"Why is that though?"

"Because people have been brainwashed into believing that

crimes committed in the name of democracy are 'necessary political manoeuvres'. Nobody has ever managed to send as many people to prison or as many innocent people to the gallows as our friend 'Freedom' has, in the same way that a million more atrocities have been committed in the name of God, and not, oddly enough, in the name of the Devil."

"That's a very pessimistic outlook and I've also noticed that you can hardly walk today," the girl noted. "Is there something wrong?"

"What's wrong is that I've reached an age where the ghosts of my past are coming back to haunt my future. It's sad to get old, but even sadder when the only thing ageing is your skeleton. Logically both body and mind should deteriorate at the same time, but unfortunately it's not like that. I've got so many things left to do and right now I'm lacking the strength to do them."

"You've still got a lot of fight in you!"

"What more would I want!" she replied bitterly. "And talking of wars, have you read what happened to that ice-cream joint on Rodeo Drive?" she nodded her head and continued, "It would seem that the rats are starting to destroy each other."

"Are you surprised?" the girl asked pointedly, "Or am I mistaken that your call to Sicily had quite a lot to do with all that..." and still waiting for a reply she added, "Why did you do that?"

"I needed to confirm a theory."

"And what's that?"

"That some bastards can be worse than even a bastard like myself could ever imagine them being."

"I love it when you are so eloquent!" the Iraqi girl said sarcastically. "Would you mind being a little clearer?"

"All I did was set the bait and I'm happy to know that there's been a bite. Far too often a lie leads to the truth."

"And what was this lie?"

"That Al Rashid doesn't exist."

Salka Embarek was becoming increasingly perplexed, as she put her paper to one side in order to concentrate more on the subject in hand.

"And do you think that the truth exists?"

"Of course!"

"So the story you gave to Tony Walker, informing him that Gigi Trotta had killed Kosinsky was a lie?"

"Only one part of it: Gigi Trotta killed Vincent Kosinsky, of that I am sure, but I suspect that he did it because he was ordered by someone high up in Dall&Houston to do it, who wanted to get rid of one more member of the board of directors. I suppose they must have made a pact that the contents of the casino's famous safe box would be shared out, but Gigi didn't fulfil his side of the bargain and kept the diamonds."

"How did you reach that conclusion?"

"Because I was the one that tipped off Dall&Houston about the diamonds and whoever killed Gigi did so because they felt cheated and took immediate action. So logically it can't be anyone other than a member of the company, who knew about it from Tony Walker."

"Peter Corkenham?"

"It's a possibility..." the old lady admitted, "Although it could be one of their collaborators or even someone higher up. Whoever it is, I expect they're feeling pretty pleased with themselves right now, because so far everything's going their way."

Los Angeles

Salvatore Aicardi knew that he was a dead man from the moment he asked the question, which he was convinced he would not get an answer to: "Who are you and what do you want?" and the boy sitting opposite him, who was filming him with a small video camera, answered casually:

"My name is Salvatore Trotta and the only thing I want to do is avenge my brother's death. This is my cousin Benito Trotta."

People only tell you their names and surnames so readily if they know you will not live to tell the tale.

So he reasoned that the best thing for him to do would be to collaborate, since he was well aware that the Sicilians knew how to make somebody talk, and he would rather not be tortured first.

"I was made to do it," he finally mumbled.

"Made to do it?" his captor said, sounding a little surprised.

"What do you mean when you say were made to do it?"

"There are times in your life when you have no option but to do something that is asked of you, and it was one of those times."

"Explain yourself!"

"The request or better put, the order, came from way up high and I'm convinced that it would have meant the end of the Aicardi in North America if I hadn't cooperated."

"And what was that order?"

"Eliminate your brother and try to recover some precious stones that apparently did not belong to him. But I suspect that the main reason was not to get the precious stones but to silence your brother forever."

"Why?"

"That I don't know, I promise you," came his seemingly honest response. "In this line of work, when someone very important gives you a job to do of a certain nature, it's best not to ask too many questions. What I did manage to find out about your brother is that he received an order to kill one of his clients, an eccentric multimillionaire that lived in the Cactus Flower. He did that well, there is no doubt about that, but he apparently couldn't resist the temptation of keeping the diamonds, which was not in his contract."

"See what my father always said..." Salvatore Trotta bemoaned bitterly. "In this business you can't betray everyone, least of all your members that are connected with government. Be faithful to those members and they will always protect you as much as they can, but if you betray them, they'll devour you."

"Your father always acted intelligently, so maybe you could make him realize that a war between the Sicilians and the Calabrians, so far from home, will only increase the amount of casualties and create orphans, for no reason whatsoever."

"You should have thought about that when you started it."

"Sure, but I couldn't do anything about it as my hands were tied. Behind the diamond story there was something much bigger at stake. Even so, I beg your forgiveness and offer your family my condolences and anything I can do to help make amends."

Salvatore Trotta took his time as he weighed up the proposal, looked to Benito for advice, but received only a blank look and a shrug of the shoulders, signalling to Trotta that ball was now in his court alone.

"Right then!" the Sicilian said. "I think that the first thing you have to do is give me the name of whoever it was that hired you and say it clearly and looking straight at the camera, so my father will be able to hear it."

"His name I don't know," the Calabrian said. "It was just a messenger that brought the envelope with that one hundred dollar note in it that means you cannot possibly say no."

"A one hundred dollar note?" a disconcerted Benito Trotta repeated, as if saying it for the first time. "Do you expect me to believe that you killed my cousin for a pithy one hundred dollars?"

"It wasn't a pithy one hundred dollars!" the other protested. "It was a hundred dollar note that was numbered."

"Numbered?" the surprised Salvatore Trotta repeated.

"Numbered..." the prisoner confirmed.

"What a load of nonsense. All notes are numbered."

"But not with this specific numeration."

"I think you must be taking the piss."

"Not at all!" his cousin Benito intervened, putting his hand affectionately on his shoulder. "You don't live here, not in this climate, so you don't know about this. But I've heard about these mysterious 'numbered notes' that have been around for about six years. They are authentic but they are not in circulation."

"So what are they used for?"

"Apparently when you are given one of them you can be sure that whoever is paying you is a very powerful figure in government. Whoever receives it, has to carry out the work they have been asked to do, then keeps the note and if one day something happens to them, like a tax inspection due that could ruin an entire business, or a drug run that gets messy, or the possibility of immediate deportation comes up, you get hold of the right person, return the note and your problems with justice are immediately resolved. That's how it works isn't it?" he said turning to Salvatore Aicardi.

"More or less," he replied. "A one hundred dollar note with a certain numeration is like a certificate that means someone very important owes you a big favour and that favour will be fulfilled at the opportune moment. Its nominal value is one hundred, but its real value is probably incalculable."

"It's like black money that doesn't leave a trace," Benito Trotta pointed out, by way of explanation. "As far as I understand it, when someone high up needs a favour that would cost too much in real terms, this note avoids the exchange of large sums of money, either from an individual or a particular department, which might lead to an investigation or an explanation being demanded. None of that is necessary with one of these very rare one hundred dollar notes."

"I understand. It's a bit like the old system of barter. I'll give you what I have and you give me what you have. You do the dirty work and I'll cover your back when you need me to."

"Quite a poignant definition."

"And what happens when the government changes?"

"It's an idea to request the pay-back in time, in case the next one isn't keen to carry on with the same game or invents another one."

"Porca Madonna!" the sour faced Sicilian muttered. "This country is full of surprises, it sure seems easier to invent a numbered note here than it does to build an atomic bomb in Iraq and still these bastards continue to convince the world that they have these bombs..." he looked the Aicardi patriarch straight in the eye in a peremptory way and said, "Where is this note now?"

His reply was disappointing.

"The last time I saw it, it was floating down Rodeo Drive and heading straight for a drain."

"That might be difficult to find now then! So you haven't got a name or a note. As far as I'm concerned you future is looking pretty bleak."

"I thought as much..." said the venerable member of the feared Ndrangheta group, who had remained admirably calm throughout the interview, considering his predicament. After meditating for a few moments on his bleak outlook, he added in an equally calm manner, "I've committed a grave error and I am ready to pay the consequences, but first of all I believe it is my obligation to prevent this from degenerating into a senseless massacre..." He pointed to the small video camera whilst enquiring, "Are you sure it's recording?"

"Entirely!"

"In that case I think we might be able to find a solution to this problem."

The following day, Salvatore Aicardi's eldest son, who was also called Salvatore, received a tape sent by Salvatore Trotta, which had his father on it, clear as day, talking directly to the camera.

"My dear wife, loving children, brothers, nephews and friends," he said. "I am speaking to you freely and I have decided to do so of my own free will. I admit that I was wrong to have taken on the job of killing Gigi Trotta, so I have decided to pay for my mistakes. My desire, and my last order as the patriarch of this family is that none of you carry out any reprisals against the Trotta family. The real culprits are too high up and therefore we cannot do anything about them without running the risk of being annihilated. It may be true that we digress from the laws they have created for their own purposes, from time to time, but we are men of honour, with a sense of moral responsibility, something, which they do not seem to possess. They might be capable of creating massacres where thousands die, but we are not. So I repeat: I order! That this act, that I will carry out with my own bare hands, puts an end to any type of confrontation between compatriots. God bless you all!"

In the next scene, Salvatore Aicardi, patriarch of the Ndranghetas in California, puts a gun under his chin and pulls the trigger.

Salvatore Trotta attended his funeral alongside various other members of the Sicilian family in Los Angeles, in order to express their deepest condolences and received not one word of reproach. Everybody knew perfectly well that the real enemy was still out there.

Los Angeles

It was the first time Salka Embarek had ever been called to her bedroom, which surprised her, but she was even more surprised when she saw how monastic and austere the large room was, in total contrast to the luxury of the rest of the house.

The old lady was lying down on the immense bed, pale, almost ashen and reading a thick book that was resting against a lectern, which she put to one side as soon as the girl came in through the door.

"Come in and close the door, darling..." she said, pointing to a chair not far from her. "Sit down there."

"Are you all right?"

"No my dear, why would I lie to you...?" and then with a brusque gesture she pulled the sheet aside, revealing her legs that were almost blue and turning black from the knee down, saying, "This is what's wrong!"

"Oh my God! Is that why you always wear trousers?"

"Yes! As you can see it's not a pleasant sight, but I think it's time you knew the truth. The way things are going they'll have to amputate my legs soon."

"Oh God, no!" the Iraqi girl stuttered, "It's not possible!"

"It is my dear; it is. From the moment I could walk this was always a possibility and I'm only lucky it's taken so long to come about. This accursed Raynaud Syndrome rarely lets any one off the hook and sooner or later it calls round for payment. First it takes the legs then maybe the hands..."

The girl was so horrified that she could barely answer.

She covered them up again, waited a few minutes for Salka to compose herself, then added:

You must understand that I'm not going to let this happen to me, I don't want to become an invalid that depends on someone else for everything, even for the most basic of bodily needs. That is no kind of life, not for someone like me."

"What are you trying to say…?"

"That I plan to commit suicide? Of course, darling! What else am I going to do! As human beings our actions and ways of thinking must be consistent, and if there's anything I've felt proud of it's having been self sufficient in everything. I'm not going to suddenly change."

"But your religion regards suicide as a sin."

"So what does it matter if I add one more to the endless list of sins I have already committed? At least this time round I'll only be hurting myself and no one else."

"What about to me. You know that I am fond of you."

"If you are truly fond of me, as I do believe you are, then I swear that it will hurt you more to see me suffer. As the blood tries to push through my veins, that one by one have started to close up, the pain will become unbearable. It will feel like someone's putting a hot poker into each and every capillary that resides in my body's extremities," she muttered under her breath and then forcing out a sort of twisted smile, she added, "That is why… because I can feel that the end is near, I had to find someone quickly who could put to good use everything that I've achieved."

"Maybe you've made a decision too quickly."

"I had to be quick and I think I was lucky…"

She tapped a file that lay on the bed next to her, saying, "My lawyer has prepared these documents and the only thing they need now is your signature. If you accept and become my adopted daughter, everything I own will become yours from the moment I decide I can't take any more. Otherwise there will be some very happy banks out there when they learn that nobody is claiming all that money."

"You could donate everything you have to charity; there are hundreds of organizations…"

The old lady stopped her with a wave of her hand, as if

dismissing the very idea.

"Most of those organisations are run by a bunch of hypocrites in ties with vicar's faces that hang on to the money when it should go to those who are most in need. I don't trust them! Anyway, if I did do that I couldn't make you into my only heiress, which is all that I actually want." She added,

"When you get the money you can give it to whosoever you want, as I'm not planning on coming back for explanations, but to be able to do that you have to accept it first."

"With all due respect to your condition and the fact that you are ill, I maintain that you are still a manipulative bastard and total son of a bitch!" came her bitter reply. "And I don't like it. I don't like it at all!"

"A leopard never changes its spots! And this animal is not long of this world and would like to go in to the next one with its legs intact because my coffin will look quite ridiculous if it measures only a meter and a half, while my legs rot elsewhere."

Her companion just stared, aghast, as if unable to believe what she was hearing, and when she finally spoke she was clearly offended.

"How can you make a joke of something that's so macabre?" she asked. "It's horrendous. And pathetic."

"Do you mean to say that my feet are pathetic. A woman with no feet would be pathetic, yes."

"If you carry on in this way I'm going," Salka Embarek threatened.

"What tone would you like me to adopt then?" came her immediate reply. "One of pity? Of desperation? Of compassion? Wouldn't it be too absurd if, having never cared for anyone, I suddenly started to feel sorry for myself. That would be a sad, miserable and embarrassing thing to do."

"You took pity on me when I most needed it."

"Wrong and you know it!" the old lady protested. "I was ready to sacrifice you without a hint of remorse and if things had gone to plan and the plot had not been discovered at the last minute, you'd be dead. Luck was on your side, not I."

"I hate you when you turn yourself into this soulless witch. Deep down you're not like that, and never have been, and you know it. Your indifference, your cruelty, they are only masks that you've hidden behind since you were a young girl in order to protect yourself."

"I was a boy, not a girl, and maybe you're right, but I'm not sure. I've always been the same and it cost me less to change sex than it would to change my soul…"

She gave her the file and pointed to the door. "For now it's best that you go off and study these documents and make a decision as to whether you're going to sign them or not and do it quickly, because I can't feel my feet any longer, all I can feel is a fire burning me from the inside out, as if I was the new Joan of Arc."

"But how will I manage without you, with all that money that you are leaving me in a country that I hardly know?"

"You've got more experience than most people do at my age and if you sign these papers you'll have more economic means and a bigger team of people than almost anyone, anywhere. I've tried to teach you what I know, my people don't need to be affected by who is in charge and it will be up to you how it's managed. Tell me, who has ever offered you so much in exchange for so little?"

"Nobody, of course, but it's not that that worries me. I'm not sure I have what it takes to assume all of this responsibility."

"For better or for worse, that is something you'll only find out when you've got one foot in the grave my dear. Only then will you be able to look back and decide whether or not you did it well, because life cannot be judged in fragments, but only as a whole. You can keep what I'm going to leave all for yourself, or use some of it to help rebuild your town and give it to those who need it, in the name of justice. That will be your luxury, although

I do understand that it will also be your burden."

"Too heavy a one."

"I don't deny it, and you can start practicing for it by picking up that black phone there and calling the embassy for the Democratic Republic of Congo in Washington."

Congo

A Herculean Congolese man, weighing almost one hundred and fifty kilos, with a wide smile and very white teeth, shook Marcel Valerie's hand so forcefully that he nearly broke it, sat down heavily in the nearest chair in front of his desk and said, as if he were merely referring to the weather:

"Good day! My name is Samuel Ombué, and I understand that you're buying up coltan deposits that are barely producing."

"You understood correctly then..." the Belgian replied, still holding his throbbing hand. "But to be honest I'm becoming less interested in buying by the day. Where's yours?"

"Excuse me..." the Congolese man said, smiling broadly. "I'm not here to sell. I'm here to buy."

"To buy?" the Belgian repeated, clearly taken aback. "That is certainly surprising considering the current climate! But to tell you the truth I'm not that interested in selling either."

"Although I imagine that would depend on the price offered," the large man pointed out. "Everything in this world has a price."

Marcel Valerie, who was feeling increasingly uncomfortable, looked the newly arrived visitor up and down, half closed his eyes and without fully opening them up asked warily:

"And what would this price be exactly?"

Samuel Ombué took out three files from a well-worn briefcase, checked through them carefully, as if he was doing a complex sum and eventually lifted his head up and looking his host straight in the eyes, said:

"Right! According to this list that they gave me in the mine registry, to date you have exclusive ownership of thirty-four important deposits, as well as options to buy or participate as the majority shareholder in a further forty-two... Is that correct?"

"If you say so..."

"That is what they have certified. Now, they have authorized me to make you an offer you can't refuse."

"And that is...?"

"One euro."

The Belgian did not say a word, as his right leg started to tremble beneath the table and after swallowing hard, he muttered:

"What did you say?"

"I said one euro and given the circumstances I'd say it's a very generous offer."

"Circumstances? What circumstances are you referring to? One euro! Are you mad?"

"Not at all!" Samuel Ombué continued in a worryingly calm tone of voice. "What I think I forgot to mention was that I represent the Democratic Republic of Congo's government..." he placed a document on the table. "You have proof of that here."

"And what has your government got to do with all this?"

"A few days ago our ambassador in Washington received a call, followed by a detailed report from someone who has travelled across the whole of the Amazon state of Rondonia and has concluded that the coltan which is supposedly being exported from there, is in fact coming from this country."

"But that's absurd!"

"Not as absurd as it initially appears to be. According to our very friendly informer, a bunch of unscrupulous characters have been acquiring large quantities of the Congolese mineral and taking it over to Brazil, creating quite a rumpus when they're pulled over by the authorities after running aground at opportune moments. All that effort just to make the world believe that there are abundant reserves of coltan in Rondonia. In the meantime, as the price continues to fall, one of their partners, that is to say you, has been buying up our deposits pretending that you are doing so at a loss.

In many countries this practice is illegal, and if I remember rightly it's called 'dumping', although we don't use this curious term. Our penal code puts it under the title of 'Knowingly manipulating the price of things', which carries a six-year prison sentence," he smiled maliciously, before adding:

"I have been told that our judges would apply this sentence to each of your purchases, which, looking at the amounts of deposits you have bought, would mean a sentence of about four hundred years in a Kinshasa prison." He narrowed one eye as he asked, "Are you starting to get my gist?"

The Belgian, whose legs were now trembling violently, and who was sweating profusely, gulped again, and looking at the large man before him as if he were about to devour him and said:

"Before we go any further with this unpleasant conversation I'd like to speak with my ambassador and my lawyer."

"We've already spoken with your ambassador, who has decided, that for the good of bilateral relationships in our respective countries, we need to keep this from leaking out as otherwise it could escalate into an international scandal of incalculable proportions and also bearing in mind that the fight for coltan has already led to the loss of millions of lives. Your lawyer immediately renounced your defence. This is something we have to resolve here and now in the most discreet way possible. That is why I am here alone."

"But this is extortion!"

"Call it what you will, but you have two options: one of those is to sign an agreement, which means that you sign over to the government everything that you own in the Congo for the symbolic price of one euro. If you do that, a boat will be waiting for you on the jetty that will take you and your beautiful Belgian friend to the other side of the lake, where in an hour or so you'll find yourselves in Rwanda and safe from harm. If, however, you decide not to comply and remain in Bukavu, then you'll go straight to prison and it is highly unlikely that either of you will ever come out alive."

"You must understand that I cannot make such an important decision by myself. I need to talk first with the people that have invested exorbitant amounts of money into this business."

"Which makes me exceedingly happy because it means at least some of the money they earned from Iraq, they've spent on our expensive mines and which our government will be now be the owners of at a modicum of the price. It really is too generous a gift."

"It would appear then, that you already know who they are."

"I have been informed of that, yes."

"And that doesn't worry you?"

"On one level...!" the Congolese man admitted. "We are aware that if they are capable of inventing a war in Iraq in order to gain control of nine per cent of the world's total petrol reserves, then they are also capable of inventing another war here in order to gain control of eighty per cent of the world's coltan reserves."

"And are you ready to fight their armies?"

"We are putting our faith in the fact that come November, whosoever succeeds Bush will put two fingers up at them, having learnt their lesson and avoid a situation that could see a war in the Congo degenerate into another Vietnam.

"My government is open to negotiation with industrialized countries to supply them with the metal at a reasonable price, which would include the cost of providing our mineworkers with decent salaries. Before we do that, however, they will have to stop financing the countries that keep invading us and all those accursed mercenaries who keep butting in where they're not wanted," he paused as if to take air, opened up his briefcase again and put a fat pile of documents onto the table, tapping with his index finger on a space at the bottom of the first page.

"You may as well start signing now because there are a lot of documents to sign and you don't want to be caught in the middle of the lake when night falls," he said in a foreboding voice, before adding, "The Rwandan soldiers, like our own, are in the bad habit of firing randomly and without warning at people who arrive on their shores under cover of darkness..."

"But I don't have the authority to sign any of this!"

"If you are authorized to buy and register the deposits in your name then you have the authority to sell them, because so far it doesn't say that these belong to Dall&Houston, or anyone else for that matter. So according to our laws, which really are the only ones relevant right now, the deposits belong to you."

"It might cost me my life."

"If I might be so bold, I would say that it is a lot easier to get around the wrath of a businessman or an American politician, however much money it might have cost them, than it is to escape from a Congolese prison. I know from experience. I spent four years in one.

"God almighty!"

"Don't bring God into this please! I don't know much about business but this has been a bad tasting appetizer. Sometimes you win, sometimes you lose and in this case your boss has just lost."

"He doesn't like to lose; especially when it is the result of a huge betrayal..." Marcel Valerie sighed deeply and resignedly, uncapped a gold fountain pen and started signing where he was being instructed to do so.

After a while and without taking his eyes off the papers, he asked casually and without really expecting a response:

"Would you mind telling me who gave out that information on Brazil and revealed the identity of my partners?"

"Apparently it was someone whose entire family was killed by a missile in Baghdad."

"And the Congolese government believed what an anonymous informer, driven by revenge, had to say?"

"Yes, when the information made sense and cleared up some suspicions that we already had. We knew that the fall in coltan prices just didn't make any sense, and anyway there was some proof too."

The Belgian suddenly stopped what he was doing and with his pen suspended in the air, went visibly pale, shaking his head from side to side and pushing the remaining papers away.

"No!" he exclaimed, "This is too much! I can't do it."

"What are you referring to?"

"To state that the money belongs to Dall&Houston."

"You don't think it's true?" Samuel Ombué asked. "We followed the thread of where this money has come from and we know its origin. We have proof and if you deny it we can charge you with trying to obstruct the course of justice, which in the Congo is also a serious crime..."

He reached his hand out and patted the other man's hand affectionately, adding, "Sign my friend, sign. When you lose a war like this one, you should be happy you've managed to save your own skin."

While the Belgian obeyed and signed the documents with a trembling hand, the government official took out his mobile phone, punched some numbers in to it and when the other end picked up said:

"No problem, your Excellency. Mr Valerie has cooperated satisfactorily so he should be allowed to travel without hindrance..." He listened and nodded before concluding, "As you wish. Don't worry, I'll get in touch with our friend Mariel. Without doubt we owe him a lot."

Los Angeles

"Their biggest mistake was playing foul with the person who invented foul play..." the old lady began, obviously finding it harder than ever to talk, intermittently biting her lips, as if to ease the intense pain racking her body.

"To ask me, of all people, someone who has carried out some of their most treacherous missions, to try and discover who is behind all this when in actual fact the whole fiasco was something they'd dreamed up themselves, constitutes a great insult to my intelligence and I'm not going to take this one lying down."

"But when did you realize that they were behind this?"

"Not that long ago, although from the start I realized that things weren't adding up, because neither Dall&Houston nor any other company in the world for that matter would use its earnings to rebuild another country, which made me ask who was actually benefiting from all those deaths."

Mary Lacombe paused in order to get her breath back, "It didn't take me long to realize that it was probably one of them and probably someone who had the power to pull off some insider dealing. The most suspect of those being the ex-president of the company, who to all intents and purpose still pulls the strings, despite the fact that he's a politician now."

"You mean Iceman?"

"Who else? He must have realized that he wouldn't be at the top of his game for much longer and knowing that coltan was the only way he could remain omnipotent, he decided he would go for total control, which meant having complete control of Dall&Houston first, the company chosen to carry out this operation."

She raised her hands in a gesture that indicated there was nothing more to know, before concluding, "And he chose terror tactics, which have always given the best results, as his modus operandi."

"It's hard to believe that someone could be so ambitious and twisted."

"The bodies of four thousand American soldiers and hundreds of thousands of your compatriots are evidence that he exists, little one, so why would he care if another half a dozen shareholders died..." She tried to smile even though it was obvious that it required an enormous effort. "I believe that deep down, Iceman and myself are one and the same because the only thing we care about is proving to ourselves that the rest of the human race is a despicable herd of sheep, unworthy of consideration."

"Is that really what you think?" Salka Embarek said uncomfortably. "That we are a herd of sheep?"

"I used to think so, and to be honest on occasions I still think so when I look at those stupid boys letting themselves be led to the slaughter, instead of taking up arms and attacking the White House, or at their parents who should have burnt down the Capitol when a pile of barely recognizable bodies were returned to them."

"Sometimes I get the impression that all this comes down to a personal vendetta you have with Iceman."

"You might be right. He very cunningly realized that by choosing me for the task, the members of the Dall&Houston board of directors would be secure in the knowledge that he was doing everything humanely possible to catch Al Rashid. It would also mean that they would never suspect that the enemy was actually among them. All this time the enemy only ever wanted their company shares, not their heads or their money."

"Now it's starting to make sense."

"Like I said, we are very similar, except that I have one advantage over him; that I know who he is and how to find him, whilst he has no idea who I am or where to find me..." She paused briefly before concluding, "Although I am afraid that as soon as my hands start to go, I will have to admit that the battle is as good as lost."

"Is a battle that is really only about your own pride really worth more than your life?" the Iraqi girl asked.

"What little life I have left, my dear, now that my legs are useless and my hands are starting to tingle, is not worth a great deal to me any longer, I told you that. The only things ahead of me are pain, frustration, terror and impotency, which I would like to put an end to as soon as possible. Although I do admit that I would rather go out having brought down one of the most despicable people they have ever produced. And excuse me when I say they, but I was born in Cuba."

"Sometimes I wonder how you can live with such a low opinion of yourself."

"Is the lion ever ashamed of who he is, the vulture of being a vulture and the hyena of being a hyena?" she said in a flash. "Of course not! They thank nature for having made them who they are, and it's only man that knows how to make other men feel inferior because he somehow feels inferior himself. I'm not inferior, just 'different', and just because I don't feel or claim to have any morals and that I don't care about anyone other than myself, is not reason enough for me to feel ashamed of myself."

Salka Embarek took a while to respond. She felt embittered, disorientated and quite sad, unable as always, to get beyond the aggressive shield that this strange person used to protect themself with, but still desperately searching for a way into the feelings of this person, who one minute she was fond of but then despised five minutes later. Conflicting thoughts and feelings engulfed her as she whispered:

"Every night I ask myself why I remain by your side, if the only thing that you give me is luxurious life style, which I could do without, and a deep sense of unease. A few days before meeting you I felt like I was strong enough and capable enough to take on the world, having seen and lived through as much as anyone could have possibly done so by my age, but when I'm with you I become someone that on occasion I don't even recognize myself."

"Console yourself with the fact that soon you will be able to get on with your life, as I won't be around to influence it. Do remember that you will have learnt more during this time than you would have done in a hundred years. Not everyone gets to live with such a sad example of the human race, born with a rotten soul on the inside and hands and legs that rot on the outside. Can you imagine what it's like to know that part of your body is dead whilst the rest carries on as if nothing had happened?

"Shit!" she exclaimed. "Me lying here in this bed while that son of a bad bitch is giving out orders," she gestured to her black telephone. "Get me Tony Walker!"

Congo

Only forty minutes or so had gone by, Kinshasa time, since the Congolese, Samuel Ombué had met with the Belgian, Marcel Valerie in Bukavu and it was a just before midday in New York when Mariel put up for sale a large amount of Dall&Houston shares that he had been gathering for some time.

That, combined with the fact that only some days earlier it had become public knowledge that the once prestigious company was in trouble, following the decision by some of its shareholders to sell everything they had for fear of being assassinated, provoked an unprecedented crash in the company's share prices on the stock exchange.

Soon after, news was posted on the internet that was immediately seized upon by editors all over the world containing evidence that the supposed coltan deposits in Brazil's Amazon jungle that Dall&Houston had invested billions in, had never actually existed. Apparently the whole thing had been fabricated by the Texan firm in order to rip off the Democratic Republic of Congo's government in a move that at the time had been condoned, or so it seemed, by the American government.

Some hours later, a photocopy of a document was also posted on the internet that revealed that a representative behind the scenes of Dall&Houston, a Belgian called Marcel Valerie based in Bukavu, had just handed over more than fifty coltan deposits to the Kinshasa government for the ridiculous price of a dollar and a half.

The White House sent out a statement straight away, denying that it had any involvement in the embarrassing affair and promising to carry out a rigorous investigation that would bring the guilty parties to justice, "whoever they might be".

The ruined and reviled company Dall&Houston, that had managed to fend off the flood of damming accusations following its involvement in the catastrophic Iraqi war, which to all intents and purposes had been lost, was not able to weather the new barrage of attacks that came at it from all angles.

This time the Dall&Houston boat had well and truly started sink and as the water seeped in to the meeting rooms and lifts, echoes of the drowning men could be heard in the corridors as they cried: "each man to his own".

In his luxurious office at the company's central headquarters in the heart of Houston's financial district, a dumbfounded and without doubt terrorized Peter Corkenham could not believe what was happening. After stopping any calls coming through to him, he hid his face in his hands, rubbed his eyes as if trying to erase recent events and looked up at his inseparable collaborator, the efficient and energetic Jeff Hamilton, who was sitting on the other side of the table, safe in the knowledge that he would be one of the few employees to keep hold of a job.

"I don't understand it!" he moaned bitterly. "I don't understand it. Do you understand it?"

The other man shook his head and he continued in the same tone, "When Iceman told me how 'Operation Coltan' would be carried out, I didn't think there was any way on earth that it could fail. We had the economic resources, the right people and the maximum official protection, which all pointed to us, five years from now, having control of sixty per cent of global reserves of this accursed mineral. But suddenly it's all gone haywire. It's as if we've been jinxed."

"These things happen…!" Hamilton said, more for the sake of saying something, than remaining in silence.

"What do you mean these things happen, Jeff? Don't screw around with me!" he snorted abruptly. "It's not on a daily basis that some Moorish fanatic comes along and hunts you down like pigs for the slaughter in the name of rebuilding Iraq. Accursed son of a bitch! The worst of it is that he hasn't managed to kill us all yet, but he has managed to destroy the company without us having the slightest idea who he is."

"Who cares who he is now it's got this far? It's done and dusted. What's important now is the future."

"The future?" Corkenham exclaimed. "What future are you referring to exactly? Iceman, who is once again living up to his miserable name, called me to tell me that he's got rid of all of his shares because he doesn't want to be involved in this mess, which means that knowing him, he'll be one of the first people to make sure we get in to even more shit than we already are."

"In that case we'll have to rely on the investigative commission to find out who's behind all this."

"Are you nuts?" the president of the Dall&Houston board of directors said, as if it was one of the most preposterous things he had ever heard. "What's happened is that his plans to become one of the most powerful men on this planet by gaining absolute control of a strategic mineral, have been foiled, but for the time being he is still one of the most powerful men on this earth. I'd rather die than have to confront him, because you only die once, but Iceman knows how to make you die a thousand times over."

The intercom buzzed and he pressed the button and screeched:

"I told you, I do not want to be interrupted!"

"It's just that Mr Walker assures me that he's got something very important to tell you."

Peter Corkenham swore under his breath, breathed deeply then reluctantly said:

"All right. Let him in."

A moment later the door opened to reveal a pale and haggard Tony Walker, who sat down heavily onto a chair, holding up his hand in an attempt to stop them from asking him any questions while he tried to recover his breath. Once he had regained his composure he said, "I'm sorry to interrupt! But it's really important. I've just received a phone call from Mariel who asked me to come and explain to you why all this has happened."

"Too late!"

"Maybe you'd rather not know then?"

"Of course I want to know, it's just that I can't imagine it will change anything now! The truth is I need solutions, not answers."

"I'm afraid that there may not be any solutions, but if you want to have the answers, Mariel said he started to notice that things weren't adding up from the moment he asked me to tell you about his suspicions regarding the Gigi Trotta affair, which he believed was linked to Vincent Kosinsky's death, who was killed the night after that information was revealed."

"I'm not sure where you're going with this."

"That the order to kill him, using Aicardi members, must have come from this office. At least that's what Salvatore Aicardi knew, before he blew his own head off, after he'd been forced to kill Gigi Trotta not for revenge or in an attempt to get hold of those blasted diamonds but because he was ordered to and he killed himself to make sure he never revealed what he knew."

"About what?"

"About the all the murders of the company's shareholders."

"Are you insinuating that I ordered the murders of Gigi Trotta, Kosinsky and all the other shareholders?"

"I'm not insinuating anything, my dear friend," Tony Walker said dryly. "I just want to point out that the only people who knew about Gigi Totter were us three, and I know for sure that I didn't give that order, so come to your own conclusions."

Peter Corkenham looked interrogatively at Jeff Hamilton.

"What have you got to say about all this?"

"That I don't know anything at all, so you can stop looking at me. You're the president and the only one with the power to plan something so grand. I don't even have enough money to buy any more shares."

"Something that you should be more than pleased about since they're only good for cleaning your ass with now. So if it wasn't me and it wasn't you that sent Kosinsky and the others to their deaths, who else could it be?"

"You know as well as I do!"

"It's not possible! I can't believe he's that twisted to order that we are killed off systemically just to open the way up for him to become company owner?"

"So you told Iceman the stuff about Gigi Trotta?"

"Of course! He's the one that gives out the orders."

"So, you have your answer right there..." Tony Walker said pointedly. "He's played games with you, and it's quite likely that if all this stuff about coltan had not come to light, before long you'd have joined Ed Pierce, Kosinsky, Marzan, Medrano, Callow, and the rest of your friends on the board of directors."

"Son of a bitch!"

"How stupid of me!" a seething Hamilton muttered. "To be honest, there was a moment when the thought did cross my mind that someone 'in-house' was responsible for all this shit, but I rejected the idea because it felt just too Machiavellian to be possible. I should have stopped to think. This evil man is quite capable of anything."

"You paid dearly for that!"

"The dead have paid the highest price, while we've been burned, lost our jobs and our reputations and he just carries on as impassive as ever, pulling the strings whichever way he fancies."

Peter Corkenham made a gesture to silence them, scratched his forehead in a thoughtful way, remained for a while deep in thought and then sighing inwardly he said:

"I can't let this happen. I'm not going to be used, trodden all over and discarded in the same way that he does with everyone. I'm not like that."

"But what can you do about it?" his ever faithful right-hand man asked. "You only have to dip your toe in here before he finishes you off, what with his connections within the FBI, the CIA, the Blackwaters, and all the other clandestine organizations in this state."

"He supposedly has those connections..." the president of the board of directors' said, "but I doubt he'd ask them to finish off our own people. I wonder who did it?"

"You have to find that out!"

"It's what I'd like to know..." he said swearing violently and then almost spitting, he added, "That son of a bitch, who dared to kill our mutual friend Ed Pierce in my own home! I'm going to have his guts!"

"His guts are a damn sight bigger than yours," Tony Walker pointed out. "You'll need some help. Mariel told me that if you decide to take on your boss then you have his organization at your disposal, for free."

"Mariel's never done anything for free."

"That's because no one's ever tried to pull a fast one like this before; paying him to look for a terrorist that doesn't even exist. I don't think he's someone with a sense of humor."

"And what do you think he can do?"

"Mariel? Whatever you ask him to do. We should also be able to count on help from the Trottas and the Aicardi. Iceman has made so many enemies in this country that if you brought them all together I doubt they'd even fit into one of these states."

"I think we'd be doing the world a great favour if we finished him off," Jeff Hamilton interrupted. "He's a pest to the human race."

"I just don't understand why..." -Peter Corkenham muttered to himself. "Why would someone who is at the top of the game and has everything, still try to get more money and power, at the cost of those closest to him? Is their no limit to a man's ambition?"

"Ambition, like the universe, has no limits and grows exponentially. Hitler was in charge of half of Europe but made the mistake of wanting the other half, without stopping to think that Russia had never been conquered."

"But why don't we try and turn this into Iceman's very own

Stalingrad?" Jeff Hamilton suggested. "All these goings on must have unsettled him and now would be the perfect time to attack."

"I can tell you don't really know him..." Corkenham countered. "He is so cold that nothing unsettles him. For almost forty years he's been rubbing shoulders with the most despicable politicians in the world, he has a dossier on each congress member, every senator, every judge, all the relevant military and business men, because he insists that alongside blackmail and violence, they are necessary if one is to remain at the top of the game. He says that it's the same game being played by everyone who wants to get ahead. It does my head in to think that at this very moment he's putting a contingency plan in place, because after working with him for twenty something years I know that if you take away his penknife he'll get out his sword and if you take away his sword he'll get out his gun, and if you take away his gun he'll kill you with his canon."

"And what do you think his contingency plan might be?"

"The one Iceman always has. What he can't get by being nice; he gets by being bad, because to some people he is all-powerful, with the president and the country at his beck and call. If Iraq isn't working in the best interests of our oil companies then we invade it, even if thousands of innocent people have to die. And if we don't get to control coltan by money, we'll get it through blood and fire."

Los Angeles

Salka Embarek knocked on the door gently, walked into the bedroom and found her host lying down and staring out at the balcony, watching the white clouds gather overhead as they marched in from the Pacific Ocean.

"How are you today?" she asked, sitting on the edge of the bed so that she could take one of her hands and stroke it gently.

"With a hot head and cold feet, my dear. I can't feel them any more which means that at any moment now they'll start to rot, and not because I haven't cleaned them but because they've got gangrene."

"Don't say that please!"

"What do want me to say? That I'll soon be giving Ginger Rogers a run for her money? You know full well that either I have them cut off or I die, but the worst of it is that my hands are starting to go to sleep…" she smiled to try and take the edge of what she was about to say, although in truth it was more of a grimace, "Which is why I've decided that on the fifteenth of this month, the forty-seventh anniversary of the Bay of Pigs, I'll put an end to it all."

"I can't actually believe that you've chosen a date for your death in the same way you'd choose one for a business meeting," the Iraqi girl protested.

"It is only a date, my dear. Ccoming from the person who never needed anyone, why should it surprise you that I, having always mapped out my destiny and taken on the world alone, have decided on the place, manner and moment to carry out this last bit of business." She sighed.

"I've managed to remain anonymous for almost half a century, despite having committed many great atrocities for no reason at all, so it's only natural that I should decide on the day of my own death with exactly the same ease that I have sent so many other people to their own death."

"Will it be your ego that finally carries you off?"

"And why can't it be my own faith; the strength of my convictions put to the ultimate test that carries me off?" the ailing lady enquired. "I've always hated it when people repent on their death bed and I can't stand the image of the prodigious boy returning home with his head hanging down in shame. I know that I will die on the morning of the fifteenth and I will die with my head held high, like the despicable son of a bitch that I have always been and of which I have always been proud."

"In that case what the hell have I got to do with all this?" she asked, still desperately trying to understand why this strange person behaved in the way that she did.

"What do you want me to say? The pharaohs were buried alongside all of their accumulated wealth, unaware of the fact that their tombs would be ransacked and their bodies pushed to one side whilst their useless treasures were stolen. There isn't a cemetery big enough in California to bury me alongside everything I own, which means I'll have to leave it to someone and you seem to be in the right place at the right time, which in this life, tends to be a win-win situation. Great geniuses have failed by not complying with the two basic rules: time and space."

She coughed a few times, bit her lips hard, as if a searing pain was passing through her body, then in what seemed like an enormous effort, pressed a bell and a few moments later the door opened and a tall impeccably dressed man, with a neat, white beard walked in. He acknowledged the two of them with a slight nod of his head, before sitting down automatically, as it seemed he had done many times before.

"This is Alan Spencer, my lawyer and the one responsible for carrying out your adoption," the owner of the house said. "He enjoys my total confidence and will advise you on anything you want. To make things easy, I have asked him to sell the film production company and the cosmetics company, which only acted as cover-ups, but they really only created more headaches than they did actual benefits.

"Alan will act as administrator, thereafter, for the buildings, the portfolio of shares and the current accounts, which means that all you have to do is pay him ten per cent of profit increase every year and that'll keep him happy. For the house employees, their salary will go up by ten per cent each year, as long as they continue to be as efficient as they are now and they respect you as they have respected me…"

She pointed to the newcomer and said, "If anyone disobeys the rules or lacks respect at all, then they are out on their ear, as everything must continue as if I was still here. And as for me, my last wish is that I am cremated and my ashes are kept safe until Castro dies. The day he dies, I would like my ashes to be taken to the house where I was born and buried in the garden. When I was forced to leave there, I promised I would return, and I always keep my promises."

Both Salka Embarek and the lawyer listened in respectful silence, conscious that they were hearing the final wishes of someone who had arrived at the end of a very long road from which there was no return. The face of the old woman was lined with pain, a pain that consumed her day and night; physical manifestations of how the illness was torturing her. There is a time when an intelligent being has to admit that their time has come and Mary Lacombe was a particularly intelligent being.

After a pause, during which time she took several breaths, nervously, almost as if she was scared that the air would not reach her lungs, she gestured with her hand for the lawyer to leave, and only once she was sure that he had left the house and closed the doors behind him, did she turn round to continue, falteringly:

"All my life I have been obsessed with making my business untouchable and I've achieved it, because I very much doubt there's anyone else who has committed as many crimes as I have without ever having paid for them. Be sure, however, that I leave this world without the slightest bit of remorse and the only thing that bothers me is that I may have to die knowing that I didn't have time to finish off the only other human being alive who might be worse than me."

Texas

A car pulled up to the doors of the imposing mansion that looked like it was being watched by two dozen or so heavily armed Blackwaters.

Peter Corkenham got out and three bodyguards searched him, then led him through a side door and through a metal detector, after he had emptied his pockets of any metal objects on to the table.

He collected his belongings and followed the guards into a luxurious salon, where a man of about seventy, wearing an elegant silk gown, was sitting on a sofa. The man gestured for him to sit down to his left, dismissing the others with a wave of his hand. They left, closing the door behind them respectfully.

"Good afternoon, Peter…!" the owner of the house said with fake affection. "I needed you to come over urgently as I think we need to clear up a few things before it's too late."

"Too late for what?" the newcomer enquired.

"Who knows! A lot of things have happened that I imagine will have affected you and I wanted to know what line of call you'd be taking with all this and I was worried that you might do something that you'd later regret."

"What kind of something?"

"You tell me! A drink?"

"No thank you. Can I smoke?"

"Of course!"

The president of the now almost defunct Dall&Houston took out a leather case with a selection of cigars inside and was about to take one out, but hesitated, offering one first to his companion, who took one out saying:

"I don't know how you do it, but despite the embargo you always manage to get the best cigars made in Cuba."

They lit them, looked at each other in silence and then the man in the silk robe started to talk again:

"I sincerely hope you understand that this has all happened in order for this country to remain a super power," he started, with the customary calm of someone who had earned his peculiar nickname. "We lost the petrol war, the Japanese make better cars, the Chinese make products at a price we can't compete with, the dollar is falling by the minute, and the exchange is collapsing, which means that if we had lagged behind in the area of communications we'd soon have become a second rate nation."

"All of that I understand," came his honest reply, "But what I don't get is why the control of coltan has to be managed by private companies and not the government."

"Governments change, my dear friend, and nobody knows what those dammed democrats will do if they win the elections. This cigar is strong!" he muttered. "A little spicy, but excellent..." He breathed in sharply, exhaled the smoke and asked, "Do you think an African country would choose a white man as their president. Would a country that was mainly Muslim accept a Christian head of state, or the Chinese, Koreans and Japanese choose a government from a different race?"

"I doubt it."

"I am absolutely sure they wouldn't, but in November a black man might win the elections in a nation that is mainly white and could be invested with supreme world power, by popular choice."

"It looks like he's on the right path," he nodded.

"Which only makes me think that deep down we white people are either the stupidest or least racist of everyone, in a world that is stupid and racist, and that unsettles me."

"Or maybe we're just trying to admit that we've made mistakes and that when faced with a difficult situation, we are capable of finding solutions, irrespective of the colour of our skin," Peter Corkenham pointed out. "Let me tell you a well-known fact; that in politics, past error can often be more informative than present day certainties. Neither do I believe that Obama will get in due to efforts of the Democrats, but due to the incredible amount of stupid things your Administration has done, which has ended up alienating all of your supporters."

"I'll bear that elemental lesson in mind, but for now I am certain that the only way we'll recover our power is if we manage to dominate the world of communications. These days there are more addicts completely plugged in to their mobile phones or the internet, than there are heroin, alcohol and tobacco addicts combined. This has happened in just twenty years. Try, just try and imagine a world without mobile telephones or computers."

"I don't think I can."

"Nobody can then."

"And what do you plan to do about it? It was almost within reach. But unfortunately our magnificent plan has been foiled, so we'll just have to start all over again."

"How?" Peter Corkenham asked. "By invading the Congo?"

"Oh good God no!" Iceman exclaimed. "We've done enough invading! Or, better put, we don't plan to be directly involved in any more invasions... We're coming up with another plan."

"Does that also include assassinating your friends?" came his angry reply. "If I remember rightly, Ed Pierce was one of your preferred golfing companions."

"And very amusing too. He told fantastic jokes, but there are times when special circumstances dictate that friendship has to take the back seat."

"Did I also belong to those special circumstances?"

"Of course not! As head of the company you were indispensable, but the truth is that you no longer are, and if you take one false step then not only you, but your entire family will pay for it." The owner of the house smiled purposefully, before concluding, "That's why I asked you to come here: forget about everything that's happened, find a nice spot in a country far away, and spend the rest of your days in peace so that I won't be forced to take more drastic measures. You've got a beautiful wife and three adolescent children. Don't mess up their future."

"Thank you for being so honest with me, although to tell the truth I'm not surprised.I expected something of the kind, but perhaps not expressed quite so crudely."

"Better that way don't you think? My final offer is one hundred thousand dollars a year and one per cent of the Texas Strategic Mineral, a company that we've just created that covers all activities related to coltan and which should be up and running within the month. You take it and disappear or you leave it and…"

"…and you disappear as well but this time for ever, is that it?" Peter Corkenham finished off for him.

"I did not say that."

"But you are thinking that. I know because I've known you for too long, which brings me to the conclusion that sooner or later you'll send someone over to finish off the work. I don't want to live with the sword of Damocles hanging over my head and waking up every morning thinking there's an assassin in the bathroom."

"Oh come on Peter! Don't be so melodramatic. You're exaggerating." He forced a laugh.

"I'm not exaggerating, and you know it. Your people will go after me and they know how to do a good job that is for sure. Every assassination gets that personal touch doesn't it, leaving everyone left to look on with real admiration.

"Anyway, before I give you a definitive answer to you proposal you might like to know about a few very useful things that I have learnt since all this happened, which I previously knew nothing about and that I think you might be interested to hear of."

"For example?" Iceman asked sarcastically.

"That the sophisticated poison that you used to finish off

Kosinsky with, extracted from a frog that is called something like an Epidobates Tricolor, does not only work by injection or through the skin..."

"But what...?"

"That it is also lethal, although it takes longer to take effect, when inhaled."

"What are you trying to say?"

"That as you only just pointed out yourself, these cigars are a little strong and slightly spicy... That is because they've been impregnated with an unusual substance that..."

"You are not trying to insinuate that...?"

"That in a few minutes our vision will go cloudy, our arms will start to feel as heavy as lead and the world as we know it will start to disappear in front of our very eyes, little by little..." Peter Corkenham smiled in quite a disturbing fashion as he pointed out, "But my soul is happy because I will be totally certain that my wife and children, the nation and the world will be safe from the evil machinations of the most incredibly callous, son of a bitch I have ever known."

Iceman threw his cigar away from him in a horrified gesture, exclaiming:

"It's not possible...! It's not possible! You're lying!"

"In death, especially when it's your own, one never lies, dear man," came his serene response.

"You are taking the..."

"You wish I was, but I've never been so serious."

"You're just trying to shock me."

"Wrong...!" Corkenham countered. "Your pig face is starting to look a little blurred and now it looks more like boar in agony... and now I can't move. Why don't you get up and ask for help?"

The owner of the fabulous mansion, who thought of himself as the most influential man in the world, made a huge effort to get up but fell back like a puppet who had had his strings cut.

There the two of them remained, stretched out on their chairs, staring out without seeing, as dribbles of spit ran slowly down their chins.

California

It is surprising that, despite the fact that there is a peace process underway and a massive presence of 17,000 UN "Blue helmet" troops, General Nkunda has started up a rebellion in the Democratic Republic of Congo. It is not the first time this has happened: he was the first in line during the Congolese Tutsi uprising in November 1996, which ended in May 1997 with the Mobutu Sese Seko regime.

Nkunda was also part of an attempted coup d'etat by the Tutsis in August 1998 against Laurent Kabila, who was no longer in favour with his patrons, Uganda and Rwanda, or the more radical American sectors, which led to a bloody civil war.

The current uprising headed by General Nkunda, who is in charge of Brigades 81ª and 83ª of the DRC army, which accounts for about 8,000 armed men, started up a few months ago, but in the last few days, following the fake Brazilian coltan scandal, it appears to have intensified.

United Nations aeroplanes have been taking soldiers and military supplies to the army that supports Kinshasa and artillery helicopters from the DRC, made in Russia, have bombed rebel positions. Official sources say that about one hundred rebels have died, but there is no external confirmation of these figures.

The fighting has forced an exodus of the civil population, already torn apart by war, hunger, illness and violence, in all of the conflict zones. Thousands of them have crossed the border to Uganda in fear of their lives.

Nkunda accuses the Joseph Kabila Government (son of Laurent Kabila, assassinated in 2001 by coltan traffickers) of supporting the Hutu rebel's Democratic Forces for the Liberation of Rwanda and its Interahamwe ("those who fight together"), responsible for the genocide of 800,000 Tutsis and moderate Hutus in the Spring of 1994. The rebel General believes that this support threatens the security of the Congolese Tutsis. Although no one has said so, it is more than likely that Nkunda has Rwanda's support, if not its blessing and whose army is the strongest in the area, made up of strategic mineral traffickers and radical North America groups. After the 1999-2003 war, Rwanda ended up with a country 14 times the size of the DRC.

This new crisis in the Congo has attracted international attention because the fighting is close to the Virunga National Park, where the mountain guerrillas live. An estimated seven hundred species live between the borders of the Democratic Republic of Congo, Rwanda and Uganda, and just recently, nine were found dead, killed by Nkunda forces. The protection of these gorillas was headed up by the American zoologist Dian Fossey, who was assassinated in her Rwandan home in 1985. Once again, coltan fever appears to be marking the destinies of both human beings and wild animals alike.

She put the paper to one side and sat looking across the immense ocean that stretched out before her.

She would like to have discussed the disturbing article and how once again the Congo was descending into war, with somebody, but there was no one around to discuss it with. True to herself and her word, on the fifteenth of April, on the anniversary of the Bay of Pigs landings, Mary Lacombe, previously known as Mauro Rivero and also known as Mariel, swallowed a cyanide capsule, one that he had been carrying around with him since the day he decided to betray the Cuban exiles, and his ashes were now being kept safe until they could be buried in the garden of her old house in La Havana.

Since that day, Salka Embarek had wandered through the rooms and gardens of this fabulous mansion on the coast of California, like a ghost, without her old patron, without any family, without friends and with only the company of a dozen servants and a lawyer who appeared from time to time with a briefcase full of cheques or documents to sign.

Instead, she found refuge amongst the enormous collection of books in the gigantic library and sought distraction by watching all of the latest films on a big screen that was in there, as if she were alone in a large cinema.

Always alone.

Alan Spencer offered to organize dinner parties so that she could meet people and even suggested she went on a pleasure cruise where she would, he insisted, meet other interesting people. But the Iraqi girl felt that she needed this time to come to terms with who she was and above all who she planned to become in the future.

On several occasions she had gone in to the office on Mac Arthur square, where Mariel, in his day, had carried out all his work to do with the Corporation. But once there, all she did was check that she knew how to work the complex machinery, but she never did anything beyond that.

She sat there, contemplating the rows of computers and wondered to what end Mariel had employed all of his superior intelligence, his incredible astuteness and amazing capacity to work.

All for what?

Probably to fill up a life that lacked meaning.

Maybe in order to escape madness.

The mind of that man-woman, who had never loved or suffered as either a man or a woman, was touched with a genius that often bordered on madness, as is so often the case with exceptionally gifted people.

During the time that they had spent together, particularly those last few painful days before she took her life, Salka Embarek had been able to make a more thorough dissection of this personality, this person who repented of nothing, who had taught her so much, but above all had shown her how not to go about one's life.

It was her very harshness, which she so strictly applied to herself, the precision with which she carried out her criminal activities, the depth of her thoughts, once the cynical barrier was dropped, alongside a strong cultural heritage, that combined to make Mary Lacombe the perfect teacher and the one to open the eyes of a poor girl, who was still very unsure about her role in life, to the world around her.

Salka was rich. By an absurd twist of fate she had become rich, immensely rich! Although maybe not so absurd when you consider that it is generally only destiny that makes human beings incredibly rich or terribly miserable. Moreover, 'luck' and 'destiny' are like a pair of stupid lovers that wander where they will, handing out charms or curses randomly, devoid of any sense of justice.

As the old lady used to say: "Luck is very scarce, and even scarcer are those that deserve it, which makes it rare that the two ever coincide. It is more likely to fall into the hands of those that do not deserve it, as there are infinitely more of them around."

She had thought long and deeply about what she should do with this dirty, blood money, but so far she had been unable to make a decision.

Maybe she should wait until things calmed down in Iraq and then she could go back and reinvest it in rebuilding part of what that accursed war had destroyed. But to do that now would be like throwing it away as nobody could guarantee that tomorrow a stray missile or car bomb would not smash it all to smithereens once again.

The wounded needed hospitals, the orphans needed homes, the homeless needed a roof over their heads, and the hungry needed food, but while the invading troops continued to patrol the streets of Baghdad, the money that might have been used to alleviate all this suffering, would just remain in a bunch of anonymous banks, still benefiting the very people behind this horrendous tragedy.

She asked Alan Spencer if there was any way that she could adopt any of the homeless girls that now wandered the bombed streets of her city, and bring them to live in her mansion, but his reply was dispiriting:

"A young, single girl cannot adopt, and if you even attempted to, it would spark a rigorous investigation and one which you would be best off without," he warned her dryly. "The laws of this country are very lax when it's the children that kill their parents, but very rigid when it comes to us saving them. That is the way of the world!" Usually dry to the point of humorless, he made an exclamation that feigned ironic amusement.

"It should come as no surprise then, that these days society is made up of many individuals who answer only to themselves and who live by their own sets of rules, since when all is said and done they are simply a product of the times of they live in."

Just as the lawyer said, Mariel was like a compendium of the times, of its brutalities and injustices; a mirror to the arbitrary nature of the world that surrounded him; the tiny piece of metal that you would find at the bottom of a melting pot that had been filled with human defects.

His indifference to pain mirrored the indifference of the majority; his cold heart was something shared by many others; his egoism, the common denominator of his species; and his ability to rob, lie and betray, something that if you took a good look around, was shared by many.

He should be perceived, as he himself often said, not as "the worst example of a human being" but as the real essence of what a human being actually is.

If aliens were to come down in search of a perfect example of the human race, the ruling race on planet earth, then Mariel might well have fitted that description.

This girl, who was now heiress to a great fortune, had no idea what to do with all the tarnished, blood stained money that she had been left.

Until one day she got a message that Tony Walker was trying to make contact with Mariel.

She looked for his black telephone, which had so many security systems set in to it, with so many diversions set on top that they were almost impossible to access, and called him.

"What's happened?" she asked

"I need to talk to Mariel," came his immediate reply. The other voice hesitated before saying:

"He promised to help us and we have found out that a new and powerful company has been formed called the Texas Strategic Mineral, which looks set to start up another war."

"In the Congo?"

"In the Congo. It looks like, despite Iceman's death, somebody has decided to go ahead with it all and is running for ultimate control of global coltan reserves, come hell or high water."

"It was bound to happen. Without power or coltan they are nothing. They haven't got much time left."

"Will you help us to stop it?"

Salka Embarek took her time as she meditated upon a decision that would undoubtedly affect the rest of her life.

She knew that if she got involved with that company it would be the first of many, and would mean following the path that the old lady had wanted her to follow and that her manipulative ways would still be working, even beyond the grave.

She felt the pain she had experienced the night when a missile fell on her house, killing her entire family; she saw before her images of suffering, the thousands of children whose lives had been destroyed by the aspirations of a miserable bunch of cretins who wanted to take charge of coltan and the world, and finally said with surprising assurance:

"You can count on us. The Corporation will do everything in its power to destroy the Texas Strategic Mineral company."

She hung up, aware that she had just tied a huge rope around her neck with a heavy stone at the end of it, a noose which she would probably never be able to remove, that might well mean that she was condemned to follow in the footsteps of someone who eventually killed themselves with cyanide.

She concluded, however, that it was up to her how well those vast funds were managed and up to her to channel them into the right places.

Maybe she would never manage to destroy outright the people that were harming humanity or maybe she would. Whatever the outcome of the battle she had just began, there were of course many more unjust wars around the corner, which would lead to unparalleled depths of human suffering, over which she would have no control.

As the old lady used to say, "The worst thing about democracy is that the people who commit atrocities in its name are rarely punished".

To hang a democratically elected government would be like condemning the very essence of democracy itself, which is why so many crimes are committed under its mantel.

For a brief moment, a fleeting moment, the thought crossed her mind that the hard and loathsome life that Mauro Rivero, Mary Lacombe, Mariel, had led, actually had a purpose and a logical meaning to it; that he had spent his entire life paving this new way for her.

All too often it is the callous among us that take advantage of the goodness in others, so maybe, just maybe on the odd occasion it is right that the good among us take advantage of the evil in others.

BOOKS

O is a symbol of the world, of oneness and unity. In different cultures it also means the "eye," symbolizing knowledge and insight. We aim to publish books that are accessible, constructive and that challenge accepted opinion, both that of academia and the "moral majority."

Our books are available in all good English language bookstores worldwide. If you don't see the book on the shelves ask the bookstore to order it for you, quoting the ISBN number and title. Alternatively you can order online (all major online retail sites carry our titles) or contact the distributor in the relevant country, listed on the copyright page.

See our website www.o-books.net for a full list of over 500 titles, growing by 100 a year.

And tune in to myspiritradio.com for our book review radio show, hosted by June-Elleni Laine, where you can listen to the authors discussing their books.

mySpiritRadio